A TONY KOZOL MYSTERY

STIFF IN THE FREEZER

by
J.R. RIPLEY

Beachfront Publishing
Boca Raton, Florida

This is a work of fiction. Any resemblances to actual places or events, or persons, living or dead, is purely coincidental.

Write Beachfront Publishing and our authors at:
Beachpub@aol.com

Library of Congress Cataloging-in-Publication Data
Ripley, J.R., date
Stiff in the Freezer : a Tony Kozol mystery / by J.R. Ripley
p. cm.
ISBN: 1-892339-04-8
Fiction. I. Title.
PS3568.I635S75   1999
813'.54—dc21   98-6891
                                              CIP

Printed in the United States of America 10 9 8 7 6 5 4 3 2 1

For Grandmaman, thanks for everything. . .
and for you, shut the door. . .

ONE

Tony took the keys.

"This is it, kid," Uncle Jonathan said. "Everything's yours now. Everything." Jonathan Kozol stood in the middle of the kitchen, one beefy arm around his nephew, Tony, the other arm gesticulating like a headless cobra.

"Yeah," Tony managed to say, "this is it." Tony's eyes took inventory over a broad, windowless kitchen and storeroom, the bowels of the Dairy Delites Ice Cream Parlor and Barbecue.

A well-ordered collection of foodstuffs lined the walls along with gallon-sized plastic jugs of ketchup, mustard and relish. There was a huge island counter in the center, itself a ghastly mustard yellow in color with stainless steel sinks at either end, big ones. A boxful of lettuce heads soaked in the farthest.

The room gave up an odor of chocolate syrup and fried fish cakes.

His mouth felt as though someone had just daubed it with a gym sock. The store keys felt about as heavy as a two pound dumbbell. And Tony Kozol was feeling like a one hundred and sixty pound dumbbell himself. "What are all these keys for?"

"Oh, those? Let's see," said Uncle Jonathan, running his hand over several of the keys, "front door, back door, register, another register, safe—the one in the floor by the sink, uh, fridge I think, upstairs door, and uh, well some of those others I forget. You'll figure them out."

He patted Tony's back with a hand that held more beef than his burgers. Uncle Jonathan was a big man with a thick wad of black hair and matching black eyebrows which hung like caterpillars over the bulbous arch of his ruddy nose.

His arm swept up from his side and through the grease filled air like a field marshal displaying his troops. "Dairy Delites Ice Cream Parlor and Barbecue. You know, your aunt and I have had this place for closing up on twenty-five years. It's all yours now, boy."

Tony thought his uncle sounded wistful. "Thanks again, Uncle Jonathan," he said. "Are you sure about this though? Maybe cousin Scott would have liked the business?"

"Nah. That kid's got college up his behind. Thinks he's too good for a place like this. He's working on his MBA now and nothing's good enough for him but the Fortune 500."

Uncle Jonathan grinned then turned serious. "It takes a lot of hard work to make this place go, Tony. Me and your Aunt Louise, well, we're just too tired for the grind any longer. Not like I need to work, anyway." Uncle Jonathan laughed like he was King Midas himself. "Besides, you can't practice law can you?"

Tony winced. "No, not for now anyway," he said defensively. "I'm thinking of appealing—"

Uncle Jonathan cut him off. "Your Aunt Louise and I both want you to have the place. Besides, we've already signed the contracts. Can't argue about the price, can you? One dollar. One dollar and you've bought yourself a little goldmine, boy."

"Yeah, Uncle Jonathan. I just don't know if I can handle it. I've never run a business before."

"Nonsense, this place practically runs itself. Besides, remember that one summer you worked here part-time? It's like clockwork, you'll see."

Tony nodded, but not in agreement.

The Dairy Delights Ice Parlor and Barbecue was a sprawling barn-like restaurant. The main building rose like a stereotypic hayloft, with the red fake shingle roof to match. And the dining room extended out from there like a long flat porch, though this one was enclosed. A pink laminated plastic counter ran along the front separating the customers from the employees.

Behind that, on one side was the grill. They served the usual fast food fare, burgers, hot dogs, chili, fries. At the other end was the ice cream. They had four soft ice cream machines and countless varieties of toppings and syrups.

There was a row of stools fixed to the terrazzo along the front wall of the restaurant, like toad stools lined up beneath a cheap, sun-faded mica ledge catching the light that came in through the smudged plate glass windows.

There was a fair sized dining room comprised of a couple of dozen booths off to the east side.

Tony had eaten there often enough but never did the wish so much as bubble up that he might own the place. And now it was his, like Uncle Jonathan so inexpressively said.

"I was thinking of going back to my music —"

"Music-smoosic. You can't eat treble clefs, can you, kid? Trust me," Uncle Jonathan said enthusiastically, "fast food is where you want to be."

Tony didn't have the nerve to suggest otherwise. How could he when his Uncle Jonathan was being so generous? "When are you and Aunt Louise leaving?"

"This afternoon. Your aunt's packing the bags now."

"Sure you don't need a lift to the airport?"

"Nah, like I told you before, it's all arranged. Got a shuttle to the airport, catching the cruise ship out of Bermuda. All part of the tour package. Besides, you're the boss. Better stick around. Gotta keep an eye on things."

"And," he muttered lowly, "on the employees, if you know what I mean. Keep your eye on the register. Most of them are okay, but watch it just the same."

"Excuse me!" grunted a rough looking teenager carrying some sort of dripping metal objects.

Tony and Uncle Jonathan parted like two halves of a clamshell. "That's Joe," said Uncle Jonathan. "Dry those grease filters this time before you put them back!" screamed Uncle Jonathan at Joe's behind. "Damn kid thinks he owns the place. Just ignore him."

Tony gulped and wondered what he'd gotten himself into. Six months before he had been a modestly successful young attorney with a blossoming practice and a lovely fiancé.

Now he was contemplating running a combination burger stand and ice cream parlor and the last he heard his fiancé was in the Grand Bahamas soaking up sun and her new beau.

Uncle Jonathan took Tony's hand and shook it. "Well, gotta go. Your aunt is waiting for me. Flight leaves in an hour, you know. Gotta catch a boat out of Bermuda."

Uncle Jonathan tossed his chef's hat at Tony. "Good luck!" he shouted, backing out of the rear door.

Tony waved as the door closed on his uncle's smiling face. The ring of keys was like lead in his hands. He picked up Uncle Jonathan's hat from the floor where it had fallen and dropped it in a nearby trash barrel.

Kozol wandered out front. Uncle Jonathan's Cadillac was pulling out of the Dairy Delites parking lot and heading up Sunshine Boulevard in the direction of his house in west Ocean Palm.

Joe was wrestling the grease filters back into place above the grill.

"Did you wipe those filters down?" inquired Tony.

Joe turned and scowled. The filter he was holding fell to the grill. "Now look what you made me do!"

Kozol mumbled some apology and turned away. There was someone banging on the glass door and pointing to his watch. "What on earth does he want?"

"It's past ten," said Joe sourly. "You're supposed to unlock the doors."

Tony hurried to unlock the doors. "Good morning,"

he said to his first real customer.

"Coffee on?"

"Uh..."

"It's hot and ready!" shouted Joe. "How you doing, Abe?"

"Great."

Kozol retraced his way through the restaurant's rear and reappeared to take the man's order. "What can I get you?"

"Just give me my coffee, is all. Where's Jonathan? He owes me for a week's worth of bread," said Abe, talking around Tony to Joe.

"Hell, he's gone. Took off a few minutes ago. This is —uh..."

"Tony." He stuck out his hand. Abe ignored the gesture.

"Tony," echoed Joe. "This is his place now. Tony is Jonathan and Louise's nephew."

"Well, ain't that swell. Your uncle owes me one hundred and seventy-five dollars for bread."

"Well, I'm not sure I have that kind of money. I'll check the register." Kozol hit the key on the register and the drawer popped open with a double ring. The cash bins were empty. "Hmmm, maybe the other register."

Joe shook his head. "Jonathan and Louise clear the registers out each night. You gotta put your start up cash in fresh each morning."

Tony checked his wallet. "I'm afraid I've only got about thirty dollars. Can I write you a check?"

Abe set down his coffee and shook his head. "Forget it. Your uncle's burned me before with that routine. No money, no bread. I ain't no bank. I'm just a delivery man. I'll come by again tomorrow. Maybe we can do business then."

"Nice," said Joe as the delivery truck hurried off the lot. "What do you suggest we do with people's burgers—tell them to stick out their hands and we'll lay a fresh hot slab of meat in their palms?"

Kozol sighed. "Here's my credit card. Go on over to the grocery store and charge what we need for today."

"Okay, boss," said Joe, "but who's going to watch the restaurant? None of the other employees are here yet."

"I can handle it just fine," answered Tony. "You get going." Joe shrugged and hopped over the counter leaving Kozol to wonder if he could handle anything at all.

He took the thirty dollars out of his wallet and divided it up evenly between the two registers. At least there was change in the coin drawers. Uncle Jonathan hadn't mentioned anything about the registers.

Come to think of it, Tony had no idea if and where Uncle Jonathan kept the books and did the banking. It had all happened so fast. One minute Uncle Jonathan was sending Kozol over the legal papers to sign and the next thing he knew, he was meeting his generous uncle at the restaurant and taking over the reins of the business.

By now, his aunt and uncle were off on an extended cruise, leaving Kozol to sink or swim.

He leaned his elbows up on the counter and waited for his first customer. Abe, for all his blustering, didn't count since he hadn't bothered to pay for his coffee. There was probably a lot of free merchandise going out the door, Tony started to realize. He'd have to have a talk with the employees about that. How was he supposed to turn a profit when they gave it away for free?

A rusty old Chevrolet Impala pulled into the lot and a young girl hopped out the passenger's side. She blew a kiss to the young man who'd dropped her off and hurried inside. "You a new guy?"

"The new boss, actually," replied Kozol. "Tony Kozol."

"I'm Gloria," said the cute young blonde. She had a cheerleader's body and outdoor complexion. Her smile was two hundred watt. The girl shook his hand. Gloria's hand felt warm and soft. "Pleased to meet you. Where's Jonathan?"

"Left on a long vacation. I'm his nephew."

"Oh, cool. Wait, let me go punch in, I'm late!" She hurried off around the back.

"You work here?" shouted Tony.

"Yeah, on the ice cream side!"

Kozol heard the clunk of the time card being punched automatically in the time clock. Gloria came out carrying a white smock which she proceeded to fold and tie around her slim waist. "All ready," she said with a grin.

"Shouldn't there be more employees here?" enquired Tony.

"Well, Susan is sick, I know. Amelia's working today, I know. Then Jean is on vacation. I think Paul comes in at noon. Joe should be here though."

"Yes, we've already met."

"That's about it then, I guess. Oh, and Leilah. Hope it doesn't get too busy."

Kozol shrugged. "What are the odds of that?"

"Not much generally," replied Gloria, as she wiped down the front counter with a clean white rag. "But Saturday is usually pretty good. We'll probably be jammed."

Someone, or something to judge by the force being applied to the back door, was banging to get in. Tony pushed the lever and opened the door. So far the back door was busier than the front. He squinted in the painful Florida sun.

"About time." A slender, fair skinned girl with thick inky black hair with one braid on the right side slipped past Kozol and into the backroom. She wore a white cotton blouse and a white skirt that came to her knees. She had on those white shoes, the kind that nurses wear. "It's after ten. You got the grill warmed up yet?"

Tony shook his head. "No."

She muttered disparagingly and pulled a time card from the rack beside the ice machine. The clock went thwack as she stuck her time card in the slot. "Great, I'm late. I've been knocking for five minutes. You taking a nap or something?"

"Sorry, I didn't hear you."

"Yeah? Well, take my advice, the next time you get some spare time you think about getting your ears checked." She softened her words with a smile. "Hi, Gloria."

"Hi."

"Come on," said the girl. "We'd better get ready. Saturday's a big day. Do you have the compressors turned on?"

"Compressors?"

"Yeah, on the soft ice cream machines. It takes a good half hour for the ice cream to get up to the right consistency."

"Sorry, again."

"No problem. We'll just have to stall." She strode out behind the service counter flipping switches as she went. The soft serve machines came to life.

She turned a knob on the grill and the scent of gas filled the room. With a practiced flip of the wrist she tossed in a match creating a tiny shock wave that rolled warm, foul smelling air over his face. "I love that," she said. "Turn on those fryers, would you?"

Tony turned to the french fry vats and cranked up the thermostats. The fat was cold, white and ghoulish.

"Three-fifty will do."

Kozol complied. "Who are you anyway?" He was glad she was on his side anyway.

"I'm Leilah." She tossed Tony an apron and put another one over her own neck. She was pretty in a dark sort of way. "Who are you?"

"Tony. My Uncle Jonathan owns—owned this place."

"Tony, right. I've seen you in here a couple of times. But that was a long time ago."

"I've been busy." Being disbarred can do that to a person.

"Piece of advice, Tony?"

"All right."

"Leave the four hundred dollar suit at home tomorrow."

Kozol nodded and put on the proffered apron.

By noon the place was, as Gloria predicted, jammed.

Paul never showed up. Leilah worked the register. That left Gloria and Amelia mixing shakes, pouring drinks and fixing ice cream orders while Tony coped with the customers and helped Joe prepare the food.

"That's it," said Kozol, wiping a line of sweat from his forehead with the edge of his soiled apron. The line of customers had dwindled.

"We'll be pretty dead from three until five," said Joe, taking a stiff wire brush to the grill.

He had the attitude of Attila the Hun, but Tony had to admit to himself that Joe was a good worker in the clutch.

"Can I go on break now?" asked Gloria.

"Sure," said Kozol. "Go ahead. You don't know this Paul's phone number by any chance, do you? We've got to have more help."

"It's on the wall by the time clock," said Gloria.

Tony went to the backroom and checked through the slips of paper pinned to the cork board. He found Paul's number and after an eternity a young sounding woman answered. "Is Paul there, please?"

"Nah, he's out of town," replied the young woman.

"He was supposed to be at work today and—"

"Work? He and my parents went to Orlando for the weekend. I've got the place to myself so I gotta go, okay?"

Kozol heard giggling in the background and then she hung up in his ear. He escaped to the upstairs office, pulled back the squeaky, gray vinyl chair and sat down with a grunt. Thirty-two years old and washed up.

Ex-attorney.

The bills on Uncle Jonathan's desk looked up at him

with apparent malice. Tony rifled through the desk and found the bookkeeping ledger tucked away in the back of the file drawer. The balance showed two hundred ten dollars and eleven cents. The invoices on the desk added up to thousands. Uncle Jonathan hadn't exactly left Kozol the gold mine he had implied.

Tony made a stab at sorting through the debts and determining which were the most pressing, like the lease payment on the building due two days hence. Other bills, like the one for paper goods were three months in arrears. From the look of things, that wasn't going to change anytime soon. In the meantime, he needed help.

Kozol decided to phone a temporary work agency. As a struggling attorney without a full-time staff, he had employed them all the time. They promised to send someone as soon as they could.

The buzzer on Uncle Jonathan's desk sounded sending shock waves of pain through the fillings in Tony's teeth. He went downstairs.

The back door shook from heavy pounding.

"Someone's at the door," said Amelia, who sat sipping a diet cherry soda and skimming a Cosmo.

Kozol gave her a look then unlatched the door.

A burly, pink-skinned man with a Mohawk haircut faced him down. He wore a blue and gray pinstriped uniform with the name Axle stitched on a white patch over his pocket. "Jonathan here?"

"No, I'm Tony, his nephew. Can I help you?"

"I've got two crates of quarter pounders melting on the stoop, you want them or not?"

"Well—" Kozol did some quick calculating in his

head. This was going to cost a fortune. "How much is this going to cost me?"

"It's all paid up. Now can I bring them in?"

With relief, Tony nodded.

Axle drove a fork truck under the crates and pushed them up beside the walk-in freezer.

Joe took a look inside the freezer and whistled. "Shit's never going to fit in here."

Kozol had to agree. "Look's like we've got plenty of stock already. I'm not sure we need these burgers."

"We need 'em," said Joe. "We were on the last box this afternoon. There's all kinds of stuff in here. More than I thought. Some of it's been here as long as I have."

"How long is that?"

"About three years."

"Sign here," said Axle, extending a clipboard.

Tony obliged. "Well, see if you can make some room before those patties melt. If you see anything you think we don't need, throw it out. I'll leave it up to you."

Joe grunted and went about his business. Kozol ran back out front to check for customers. Tony was in the process of spilling catsup on his two hundred dollar loafers when he overheard a young woman asking for him at the counter.

"Sure, Mr. Kozol, he's right here," said Leilah, who stood manning the register. "You do mean Tony, not Jonathan, right?"

The girl looked at a slip of paper in her hand and nodded. "Yes, Tony Kozol. That's the name the agency told me to ask for," she answered.

Tony smoothed his apron and approached the woman.

She had long blonde hair and strong Nordic features. She looked to be anywhere from thirty to forty years old and was not unattractive. She wore a conservative blue dress with a simple silver chain around her neck. "I'm Tony Kozol. Can I help you?"

"Hello, Mr. Kozol. My name is Nina Lasher, Working Temps sent me."

"Right, of course. That was quick."

"I live close by."

"Well, listen, miss, come around back and put on an apron and Leilah can get you started."

Once behind the counter, Leilah helped the new girl into a long white apron. "Careful of that dress, honey."

"It's okay, it's not expensive."

"Have you ever done this kind of work before?" inquired Kozol.

"No, sorry—not really."

"Well, don't worry, anybody can do it. Nothing to it."

"Have you ever worked a register?" Leilah asked.

"A little. I'm a bookkeeper actually. I got laid off last month from Fidelity Bank when they merged with Orange Savings, corporate downsizing."

"A bookkeeper? Say, listen," said Tony, "maybe you could just look over the books for me first, let me know what you think."

"Well, I don't know."

"Come on," said Kozol. "You see, this is my first day running the place. I'd kind of like to get an idea where I stand. The books are upstairs, at least what I could find."

"Okay, if you really want me to."

"Great," said Tony. "Rummage around the desk for

STIFF IN THE FREEZER

anything you want. Leilah will show you the way."

The next hour passed quickly as another wave of customers hit them. When the crowd slackened Tony prepared himself a chili dog and was pouring himself a cup of coffee when Joe called from the freezer. Kozol took a quick bite of his chili dog, snatched an onion ring from the warming tray and went to see what was up.

"What is it?" said Tony, stepping into the fifteen degree freezer.

"Some of these boxes here are stuck to the boards. Help me push." Moisture had leaked into the freezer and the boxes were caked in ice, melded to the stiff wooden floor slats.

Tony and Joe pushed and kicked until the old boxes gave way.

"I want to check out what's in that last box in the corner."

Kozol grumbled. His hands and ears were numb. "Looks like you've already thrown away half the stock. Surely there's room for the burgers now. They're beginning to melt. Come on, let's get to it."

"That box takes up a lot of room," said Joe, stubbornly moving the last case of chicken patties to get to the box in the corner. The box Joe was so anxious about was nearly four foot tall and unmarked.

"May as well see what's inside," said Tony.

"It's heavy," remarked Joe, rocking the box side to side and trying to maneuver it out into the light.

One side of the box broke away and a ghostly white figure, rimed in ice fell forward.

Amelia, who had until then been watching over

Kozol's shoulder with amusement, screamed.

"Jesus!" gasped Joe, tripping over his own feet and tumbling out the freezer.

Tony stood frozen in his tracks. In the freezer was Michael Razner, the source of all his troubles.

TWO

Michael Razner. Kozol hadn't seen the son of a bitch since the hearing had ended months before.

"Want me to call the police?"

"Maybe we should think this through," said Tony.

"Think what through? You want we should sit his frozen ass on the grill and thaw him out?"

Kozol suddenly realized the horrified reaction of his customers as they carted the frozen body out the door.

"Hey, what's going o-OOOOO!" Gloria had come back from the restroom.

Tony put a hand over the girl's mouth. "Shhh, please."

"But—But...who?" she whimpered.

Joe shrugged. "We've got to call the police."

"There are a few of them sitting in booth nineteen," said Gloria.

Kozol wished they would just agree to close the box back up and shove it away in the freezer where they'd found it. If he'd found the body alone, that's just what he might have done.

This wasn't going to look good. What was Michael Razner, a notorious mafioso-type, doing in Uncle Jonathan's freezer? In Tony's freezer! "Well..."

One of Ocean Palm's finest came through the door connecting the backroom to the dining area. "Officer Keyes," announced the young officer with authority. "I heard a scream. Everything okay?"

Gloria pointed a trembling finger.

"He, uh, seems to be dead," said Kozol.

"Shit." The dark haired policeman approached the body. "Cold dead, all right. Hey, Rocky, Chris—get in here!"

What few employees Tony had were suddenly collected in the backroom. "Will some of you please get back to work," he shouted. "We might actually have a customer or two."

Though with a corpse discovered in the freezer, that wasn't likely to be the case much longer, Kozol feared.

"Wait," said Officer Keyes, "who discovered the body?"

"Me and the boss," said Joe.

"Okay. The rest of you can go back to work."

Leilah, who had appeared out of nowhere, placed her arm around Gloria and led her quietly away.

"Anybody recognize this guy?"

Tony gulped. "That's the strangest thing," he said, figuring a lie would only be found out, "I do."

Officer Keyes cocked his brow and seemed to look at Kozol with new found interest. "That so?"

"His name is—was Michael Razner."

"You mean that's the dude you were complaining about this morning. The sleazeball who got you disbarred and that's how come you ended up in this dump and—" began Joe, before Tony could shut him up. A looser cannon there never was.

"Shouldn't you be putting the rest of this stuff back in the freezer, Joe?" Kozol said, sternly. "Everything's liquefying."

"Better not touch anything just yet," said a stone-faced officer next to Keyes.

Officer Keyes and his partners moved in closer. Rocky Murchison, according to his badge, a beefy character with a weak looking chin, gently put his hand on the dead man's left shoulder and leaned him forward. Frozen blood broke loose.

Amelia, who hadn't left the room, turned a deeper shade of green and vomited up her lunch in the sink—on top of twenty dollars worth of fresh lettuce heads, noted Tony.

"This guy looks like he was popped in the back."

"Shooting?" asked Keyes.

Murchison frowned. "I'd say so, but we'll let the M.E. be the judge of that." Murchison let go of the corpse and the body fell back in the box.

Keyes shivered and eased the door of the freezer closed with his toe. "We're going to have to be careful to preserve any evidence, though I don't suppose fingerprints are likely. Rocky, watch the body, okay. And Chris, you'd better phone for a ride for our friend here before he thaws out."

Chris nodded and spoke into his shoulder mounted transceiver.

"And now, Mister..."

"Kozol," said Tony, "Tony Kozol."

"Kozol? Name sounds familiar," Murchison said. His look was quizzical and unpleasant.

"Yeah, it does," replied Keyes, scratching at his weak-looking chin. "Let's go someplace where we can talk, Mr. Kozol. I'll want a word with you next," he said to Joe, who wasn't looking so good himself. "So stick around."

Joe nodded glumly and stuck his hands in his pockets.

Tony led Officer Keyes upstairs to his office. Nina sat going over the books. In the excitement, he had forgotten all about her.

"Mr. Kozol, what—"

"Sorry to startle you miss," said Officer Keyes. "Would you mind leaving us alone? I'm sure Mr. Kozol won't mind."

Nina Lasher looked at Tony as if seeking for guidance.

"It's okay," said Tony. "There's been—an accident, and I need to speak with Officer Keyes alone for a few minutes."

Miss Lasher picked up the ledgers and headed for the door. "I can work on these just as well downstairs, I suppose."

"Better make that the dining room," said Officer Keyes.

Kozol nodded.

"Pretty cute."

"Huh?" Tony followed the sound of the temp's footsteps down the stairs.

"Your Miss Lasher. She's an attractive girl."

"I guess so," answered Kozol, though he hadn't really thought of it.

"How long has the young lady been working for you, Mr. Kozol?"

Tony leaned against the wall for support. "Her? Oh, she doesn't really work for me. She's a temp. Just came in today."

"I see," said Officer Keyes.

Tony wondered what he possibly could see.

"You mind answering a few questions?"

Kozol shook his head from side to side.

"You don't want a lawyer present?" said Officer Keyes. "Not that I'm charging you with anything—"

"Look," said Tony, feeling a sudden urge to fight back, "I am an attorney, or at least I was as you might have gathered from what Joe was rattling off about. And it's because of Michael Razner that I am stuck here, pumping ice cream and flipping burgers. So don't tell me about lawyers. I can take care of myself!"

"Yeah, so I see," said Officer Keyes. "Is that what you did? Take care of Razner? His name I am very familiar with. Local hood with connections all the way to New York from what I hear. You have a temper?"

There was a hasty rap on the office door.

"What?" shouted Kozol.

Nina poked her head around the corner. "Uh, Mr. Kozol, there's someone downstairs."

"Good, maybe he'll buy something."

"I don't know, he is acting kind of crazy and he's filthy. I think he's scaring away the other customers. Joe says not to worry about it, but I believe you should come."

"We'll check it out," said Officer Keyes with a voice of authority.

Together Tony and Officer Keyes headed back downstairs with Nina leading the way.

"That's him," said Nina. The man in question was now seated on a barstool, a generous serving of fries, a double decker cheese burger and a cola lay before him.

"Hey, it's all right," said Joe. "Like I said, it's just Roamie."

"Roamie?" said Kozol.

"Yeah. I don't know his real name. We just call him Roamie because that's what he does, roams, you know? He lives around here somewhere. He's cool," said Joe, more to Officer Keyes than his boss.

Tony tentatively sniffed the air. From the smell of Roamie he apparently lived someplace without running water. "What's he doing here?"

"Comes in every day or two," interjected Leilah. "Your uncle always gave him free meals."

"Free meals! And scaring away the paying customers to boot," he said, lowering his voice a notch. He'd seen the looks customers were giving the apparent vagrant and how they avoided eye contact with him. No one sat within a twenty foot radius. Was that coincidence?

Kozol didn't think so. "No more freeloaders and no more free food," he said in a low but firm voice. "No more free coffee, no more—"

"But the delivery men always get free coffee, cones too, sometimes," said Gloria.

Tony was firm. "No more they don't."

Joe shook his head. "Not much of a way to do business. They aren't going to like it."

"It's the only way to run a business. Look," said Tony, "this is my restaurant now, so we'll do things my way, got it?"

One by one they nodded.

"Mind finishing our conversation now?" said Officer Keyes.

"Of course," replied Kozol.

"What do I do about Roamie?" asked Joe.

"Let him finish his lunch and then tell him it is the last one he is going to get for free."

"Why do I have to tell him? He's not going to be happy."

"So? He's not even a paying customer. Listen, tell him it's the new management, a new policy."

Tony stormed into the backroom with Officer Keyes only to discover the lab team had arrived. A photographer was taking a flurry of shots of the now thawing Michael Razner. Another crew stood by waiting to remove the body. The soul, if there ever was one, had departed long ago, realized Kozol.

A grim looking man with a sunburned face, wearing a cheap department store suit strode forward. "Frank Fender. Homicide," said the man. "You Jonathan's nephew?"

"Yes. You know my uncle?" Maybe this would be a turn in his favor, Tony hoped.

"Yeah, I know him. But it's you I was looking for."

"Well, I don't know why," said Kozol. "This is exasperating. I only got here this morning. This is Uncle

Jonathan's restaurant. Maybe he's the one you should be talking to."

"So," said Fender, his eyes narrowing, "you think your uncle did this?" Fender put a hand on Tony's shoulder and turned him toward the corpse. Razner was looking worse by the minute.

"No, no, I didn't mean that. Uncle Jonathan wouldn't hurt a fly. But I'm a lawyer not a frycook and I only took over here this morning. I don't know how Razner ended up in the freezer."

"I thought you said you used to be a lawyer," said Officer Keyes.

"Used to be?" asked Fender.

"I got disbarred," said Kozol sullenly. "But it wasn't my fault!"

"I remember now," said Officer Keyes. "It was Razner who turned States' witness against you for collecting laundered money."

Tony winced. He supposed there was no reason for trying to hide the truth any longer. It had been in all the papers, and these were cops to boot. They'd find out sooner or later.

"He framed me," replied Kozol. "It was all a setup. I represented Mr. Razner in a tax case, which we won, I might add," he said proudly.

"And to show his gratitude, Razner set you up with the feds?" Fender replied caustically. "Why did he have it in for you?"

Tony hesitated only briefly, finding no way out. "He thought I was fooling around with his girl—but I wasn't. Not really. That is, she came on to me. I didn't even know she was his girlfriend at that time."

"How did it happen exactly?"

Kozol, with surprising ease, spilled his story to the officers. "Michael Razner owns a club down in Pompano, Girls Galore—"

"The strip joint?" said Officer Keyes.

"Yeah," Tony replied. "Listen, I got a call at my office that Razner wanted me to represent him in some civil cases. He was paying big money. I'd only been in practice for less than a year. Money wasn't exactly rolling in. Razner gave me a big, fat retainer.

In retrospect I wish I had never met that bastard but at the time I was grateful for the income—honest income," Kozol added hastily. "Razner had only been to my office once. He almost always wanted me to meet him at his club to discuss the case. That's where I met Pamela."

"Razner's girlfriend?" asked Officer Keyes.

"Yes, she worked in the club. One night early on in the case she came over to my table. I was sitting in the back, waiting for Mr. Razner to show up."

"What's her last name?" asked Fender.

"Brown."

Detective Fender nodded, as if committing the simple name to memory. "Go on."

Tony nervously bit the inside of his cheek, then forged ahead. He was sweating. "Razner was late. Pamela came over to my table with a glass of champagne in her hand. She took a sip and handed me the glass."

"You screw her?" asked Detective Fender.

"We went out a few times," said Kozol, visibly fidgeting.

"I asked if you diddled her," repeated Fender.

"I didn't even know she was Razner's girl!" Tony said, his voice involuntarily rising several notches.

"Bingo," said Detective Fender, with a nasty laugh.

Kozol scowled.

"So you had an affair with Michael Razner's girl-friend," said Detective Fender with something approaching respect in his voice. "Wouldn't be the first time two men fought over a woman and only one side lived to tell about it. Add one disbarred lawyer to the mix and I'd say the D.A. is going to be one happy puppy."

"Not so fast," said Tony, visions of prison time dancing through his head. "What about Razner's wife? He was married, you know."

"Yeah, well, we'll look into it," agreed Fender, though he did not show much interest.

"Anything else, Frank?" asked Officer Keyes.

"Nah, you can clean up this mess," Fender said, stepping over a box of once frozen onion rings lying in his path. "You own a gun?" he said turning to face Kozol.

"No."

Fender looked from the corpse to Tony. "Don't go anywhere I can't find you," he said on parting.

THREE

Kozol dragged himself up the stairs to his office, ignoring the commotion all around him. All he wanted to do now was settle back in that old gray chair of Uncle Jonathan's and shut his eyes. It was too much to hope that this was all a dream, but maybe he could sleep and pretend that it was.

"Oh, Mr. Kozol."

Tony groaned. "Yes, Miss—"

"Lasher."

"Right, Lasher." Kozol wished she would disappear, along with all his problems. Not to mention she was sitting in his chair.

"With everything going on downstairs, I thought it would be okay if I came back upstairs to work."

The sleeves of her dress were rolled up to her elbows. A pencil was stuck in her hair. It looked like half the papers from the drawers had been dumped atop the desk.

Tony hoped she really knew what she was doing.

Kozol flopped down with a sigh onto the worn-looking beige sofa against the side wall of the tiny office. The room was barely ten by ten feet, not much room for two people plus furnishings. The sofa itself took up a wall.

"I can't believe this is happening." Tony ran his hands through his hair and sighed. His eyes were shut.

"You want me to leave?"

"Huh, no," said Kozol, looking at her through slitted eyes. "Unless you're afraid I'm a murderer."

"You really knew that man?"

Tony nodded. "Yeah, he set me up. Now here I am. I can't believe it. What the hell is his body doing at Dairy Delites of all places?"

"Maybe you should phone your uncle. Leilah told me about how he gave you the restaurant. Did he know the victim?"

"No, he couldn't have. At least, not personally. Uncle Jonathan knew about my legal troubles so he certainly had heard Razner's name before. But he never intimated that they knew one another. You don't know my uncle. He's a pussycat. He wouldn't know a slime ball like Razner. Uncle Jonathan and Aunt Louise are active churchgoers. He's even a member of his church Board of Elders at St. Jude's."

"I guess you're right."

"Besides, Uncle Jonathan and Aunt Louise are off on a cruise somewhere, god knows where." Tony shifted his weight on the sofa. The cheap foam cushions were unfriendly.

Kozol stared at the tops of his loafers and theorized

aloud. "I wonder if Scott—that's their son—could somehow have been mixed up in this. Scott's got a temper and I've heard rumors that he runs with a bad crowd. Likes to party. Maybe he owed Razner some money."

"You don't know where your aunt and uncle were going? Maybe you could reach them on board their ship."

Tony frowned. "I'm not sure," he said, rubbing his temples and sitting up. "I remember Uncle Jonathan saying they were going through the Panama canal. I think he and Aunt Louise were going all the way to California from there."

Kozol shook his head. "I really don't recall. I don't even know the name of the damn boat."

"Isn't there anyone at their home who could tell you? Scott?"

"No, he's got an apartment near the University of Miami. Wait!" said Tony, snapping his fingers. "I'll call and leave a message on Uncle Jonathan's answering machine."

He picked up the phone and dialed.

"Maybe Uncle Jonathan will check his messages."

Kozol listened to the phone ring four long times before finally being picked up by the answering machine on the other end. "Hello, Uncle Jonathan, this is Tony," he said. "Listen, if you get this message there has been a bit of a problem at the restaurant. I'd appreciate it if you would give me a call at your earliest convenience, thanks. And I hope you and Aunt Louise are having a terrific time."

Kozol decided that it would be in his own best interest not to say too much about the particular circumstances of his dilemma and rather leave things vague. If he told

Uncle Jonathan about a dead man being found in the Dairy Delites freezer his uncle might decide never to call back, assuming he got the message at all.

After all, Uncle Jonathan and Aunt Louise were on their first real vacation in twenty years, thanks to Uncle Jonathan's unexpected inheritance. Tony could understand that Uncle Jonathan would not be quick to let some far away unpleasantness spoil it so soon.

"What about the finances," asked Kozol, turning to face Miss Lasher, "any luck?"

"Not much, I'm afraid. Everything's a mess." Miss Lasher ran her hand through a stack of invoices. "These are all past due, by the way."

"Any sign of a checkbook?" asked Tony, hopefully.

"Yes, but it hasn't been balanced in ages. At best I'd say there's a couple hundred dollars in the business account."

"And at worst?"

"You're overdrawn. As sloppy as the books are, I wouldn't be surprised. You may want to think about making a personal loan to the business."

Kozol scowled. "I've been doing that all day."

"It was only a suggestion," said Miss Lasher, demurely. "I'm only trying to be helpful. Perhaps I should go back downstairs now and help out there."

"I'm sorry," said Tony. "Look, it's been a pretty bad day all around. I'd appreciate it if you'd work on things here some more."

"To tell you the truth, Mr. Kozol, I shouldn't be doing this at all. The agency would have a fit if they knew. They get a lot more money for this kind of help than they do general restaurant labor."

"What exactly is the agency charging me now?"

"Fifteen, I'd guess. I only get eight of that."

"Tell you what," offered Tony, "at the end of the day I'll phone the agency and tell them I don't need you any longer. Then I'll pay you say, twelve dollars an hour to work for me until we get this sorted out. What do you say?"

Miss Lasher pursed her lips. "Well, it doesn't seem quite honest."

"You'd be doing me a big favor," Kozol said, striking what he hoped was his most charming pose. "You see what kind of mess I'm in here."

"Well—"

"I didn't kill anybody, believe me."

"That's for the police to figure out," Miss Lasher replied. "But I could use the money—"

Tony took that for a yes. "Great. I'll make all the arrangements when I get back. Right now I've got to go see somebody." He turned and hurried down the stairs. He had an idea.

"Going somewhere?" barked Officer Murchison.

Kozol turned around at the back door and took his hand off the knob. "I need to go see someone," he managed to gulp.

"Like a real lawyer?" chided Officer Murchison.

Tony made a face. "No."

"The only place you're going is downtown. I've got orders to bring you in for more questioning."

"Do I have to?"

"Might be better for you if you cooperate, Mr. Kozol."

"But the restaurant—"

Murchison nodded his head. "Business is closed for the day. Got a warrant to search for a gun. We've already taped off the premises and sent most everyone home. The girl, Leilah is here and the other kid, Joe. Leilah said she could lock up."

Tony sighed. Life was definitely pounding on him this day.

"Shall we?"

Kozol nodded and was escorted ignominiously into the back of a late model Ford cruiser. Officer Keyes patted Tony down and pushed his head into the car.

Why do the police always have to do that, wondered Tony? Did they think that civilians bumped their heads every time they got into their own cars without a friendly officer of the law to protect them from themselves?

Officer Murchison drove. Officer Keyes sat next to him.

¤

The Ocean Palm Police Station was a model of modern Florida design, sleek, low and nearly all glass. Low maintenance xeriscaping surrounded the exterior, mostly liriope and mulch.

The officers led Kozol to a tiny, interior interrogation room. There were no windows here. A fluorescent light gave off a pinkish glow.

"Wait here," said Officer Keyes.

Tony paced around the small laminated table. Several minutes later Officer Keyes returned with Detective

Fender.

"Sit down," said Fender. "Thanks for cooperating with our investigation, Mr. Kozol."

Tony sat. "Happy to oblige," he said, though hardly meaning it. "Truth is, I don't know much."

Officer Keyes set a small microcassette player on the table.

"You mind?" asked Detective Murchison.

"No," said Kozol.

"Fine." Murchison turned on the recorder. "We are recording this conversation with your permission, Mr. Tony Kozol?," he reiterated for the tape.

"Yes," Tony said loudly.

"Do you own a gun, Mr. Kozol?"

Tony nodded his head no and then remembered the tape recorder. No," he replied.

"And when was the last time you saw Michael Razner?"

Kozol rubbed his temples. "I can't remember—"

"Yesterday?" asked Fender.

"No, definitely not."

"Last week?" asked Officer Keyes.

"No, not since the hearing regarding my disbarment," answered Tony.

"Three months ago. You were seen arguing violently with the victim at his establishment, Girls Galore, by several persons, who are willing to swear that you threatened Mr. Razner and created quite a scene until a couple of his goons threw you out. This was after you were disbarred."

So they had already been checking on him. "I was

angry," said Kozol. "His lies cost me my job. Hell, my career. Wouldn't you be angry? But I didn't kill him. I'm not stupid."

"Never accused you of that," replied Detective Fender rather ominously.

"Listen," said Officer Keyes, obviously taking up the role of good cop, "we only want to get to the bottom of this murder. And the body was found in your place of business. The more you cooperate, the quicker things can get back to normal there. Stuffing a corpse in with the french fries isn't going to be good for your establishment's reputation, Mr. Kozol."

"Where were you Friday evening?"

Tony thought. "Home."

"Have any company?"

"No, I watched t.v. Went to bed kind of early. Why?"

"What did you watch?"

"Sitcoms," said Kozol, squirming.

Fender laughed. "A little low brow for you, isn't it? Shouldn't you be watching Court TV?"

"What were the shows about?" asked Officer Keyes.

"I can tell you exactly what the episodes were—" began Tony.

"Doesn't matter," said Fender, shaking his head. "Summer reruns. You could've seen any of those network shows already."

"Use the phone that night, Mr. Kozol? Call anyone, or anyone call you?" asked Officer Keyes.

"No."

"You've been disbarred from practicing law. Razner turned you in—said you'd been working for him."

"He only did that to save himself and the idiot state's attorney bought his act."

"Everybody at the club says you were throwing money around on that dame, Pamela Brown."

"It's not true."

"You must have been awfully angry at Razner," said Fender. "Ruined your life."

Tony thought Fender seemed to like that.

"Mad enough to kill him?"

Kozol said nothing.

Detective Fender leaned over the table. His breath smelled of tuna fish and cigarettes. "We've spoken to Mr. Razner's wife, Laura. According to her, she last saw her husband alive on Friday afternoon. She spoke to him once after that briefly on his cell phone."

"And according to the coroner's preliminary findings that isn't out of line with when the victim could have died," added Officer Keyes.

"But I didn't even own the restaurant, don't you see? So it couldn't involve me then, could it?" Tony stated defiantly.

"When did your uncle decide to give you the business?" demanded the foul smelling detective.

"He called me about it Friday," answered Kozol. "I thought he was joking. It seemed so sudden. But then once Uncle Jonathan makes his mind up about something, that's how he is—impulsive."

"So, yesterday you knew you were getting the restaurant. Very convenient. Maybe you met Razner somewhere last night, shot him and stuck him in the deep freeze knowing full well that you could move the body later when it was convenient."

"That's a nice fairy tale, Fender. But there's one thing missing—a key. I only got the keys this morning."

"That fellow, Joe, said that your uncle kept a spare key to the place under a small stone under the air conditioner unit out back. Seems just about everyone connected with the place knew about it," Officer Keyes stated matter-of-factly, as he checked his notebook.

Tony said nothing. In fact, now that Officer Keyes mentioned it, Uncle Jonathan had told him about the key years ago and told Kozol to remember where it was in case there was ever an emergency and Uncle Jonathan and Aunt Louise weren't around for some reason.

But if Tony mentioned this little fact to the police it would only look worse for him. "Did you find this supposed key?"

Fender shook his head in the negative. "Nothing, but everybody swears it used to be there. But nobody can remember the last time they'd seen it or used it." Fender changed directions. "Have you seen Razner's girlfriend lately?"

"Haven't seen her for ages."

"Maybe the two of you planned this together?"

"Maybe we didn't," Kozol answered, angrily. Fender was fishing but Tony had to admit that the detective's hook was getting under his skin.

"You're not being very helpful, Mr. Kozol," said Officer Keyes.

"I don't have any help to give," said Tony. "But I do have a restaurant to run. Hopefully, I'll be able to open up for business in the morning if your men are done tearing up the place."

"Hopefully," said Fender with noticeable sarcasm. Fender nodded to Officer Keyes.

"That's it for now, Mr. Kozol. As you know, we expect your full cooperation," said the officer.

"I know, I know, don't leave town."

"Bingo," said Detective Fender.

¤

Tony left in a hurry. He'd never been comfortable in police stations, even when he was a working attorney. He was one of those people who got nervous any time there was a police car driving behind him for no reason at all. Kozol's palms got sweaty, his heart raced and waves of unrequited guilt washed over him.

No one had offered him a ride back to the restaurant so Tony telephoned from a pay phone outside the station for a taxi. He tried phoning the Dairy Delites while he waited but there was no answer. Hopefully, the last person out had locked the doors. The restaurant business was turning out to be more trouble than it might be worth, realized Kozol, wearily. Then again, what other options does a disbarred lawyer have?

The car and driver arrived in moments. Apparently the police were generally good for only one way trips.

"Where to?"

"Girls Galore," replied Tony hopping, in the back of the car. The cab smelled of mildew and cheap air freshener. "Do you know where that is?"

"Pompano," replied the taxi driver with a grin. He

spoke with a thick Haitian accent. "Be looking for girls, I know where some very pretties. Much closer than Pompano. You interested?"

"No," said Kozol. "I'm looking for someone in particular."

"Ahh," said the driver with a sigh of disappointment.

Tony only hoped that the someone in particular he was looking for would be there.

Kozol passed the time trying to figure out just how much money the day had cost him and wondering how long he could afford to be in business if this downward spiral continued. After news of the murder got out he figured he'd be lucky to have any customers left at all.

Maybe he would call a real estate agent in the morning and see what he might get for the place. If he could come out of it with some cash, things might not be so bad. He might even start up some other type of business, something simpler, maybe even a franchise. Tony was saved from his reverie by the taxi driver's request for money.

"Twenty-six dollars," demanded the driver.

Kozol emptied his wallet of exactly twenty-six dollars. Even after looting the register that afternoon, the cash was running dry. He couldn't afford a tip the way things were going.

The driver said nothing but flipped Tony the finger as he drove off.

The parking lot of Girls Galore was only half full. Tony looked at his watch. It was barely seven o'clock. The pre-dinner crowd would be gone. The place wouldn't crank up for business again until after nine.

The Girls Galore building was a fairly impressive, two

story, Art Deco style structure. And painted lilac one could hardly miss it. Formerly a disco, the club had flourished under Michael Razner's direction. He had known what men wanted and he saw to it that they got it.

Kozol drew back one of the sturdy double doors and entered the eternal night. A sexy young girl nestled behind a large oak desk upon which sat an incongruous looking cash register.

"Hi," she said with a paid for smile. She stood, exposing a near perfect body clad in an outfit which could have been plucked from the Victoria's Secret catalog. "Welcome to Girls Galore. There's a ten dollar cover."

Tony handed over the money and instinctively reached out his hand.

"Oh, you've been here before," said the girl.

"A long time ago."

She took Kozol's palm and planted a glowing phosphorescent stamp on the back of his hand. It was a pair of lips, full and sensuous. "Have fun!"

Tony parted the velvet curtains separating the lobby from the main room. He had decided not to ask the girl whether Pamela was working. For all he knew, Pamela would run if she knew Kozol was looking for her. Or worse, call out the goons. Then again, Tony realized with discomfort, there was no reason to think that wasn't going to happen anyway.

Kozol stood and let his eyes adjust to the room. A hardy few, horny and presumably family-less men manned the tables. A half a dozen or more girls, nude or soon to be so, mingled among the customers. Rock and roll music pounded out from the large speakers surrounding the stage as a voluptuous blonde wrapped her legs around a glistening chrome pole and rhythmically wriggled to the beat.

Tony took a seat at an empty table near the stage and ordered a beer. There was still no sign of Pamela. The dancer's moves were mesmerizing. The colored lights kept time to the music. Kozol was only half-surprised to see that Michael Razner's demise had not stopped the action. Life goes on, even for the dead.

"You shouldn't be here." A hand pressed down firmly on Tony's shoulder.

He shot up halfway, spilling beer in his lap, and turned. "Pamela."

"Sit down, baby," she whispered, giving him a push.

Kozol felt a familiar feeling coming over him, the blood rushing somewhere midway between his head and his feet. Pamela looked as beautiful as ever. Long, wavy black hair, one-of-a-kind green eyes and a centerfold's body.

All she was wearing was an abbreviated sequined silver G-string and matching silver shoes with four inch heels. Knees bent, he stood eye-to-nipple with Pamela's bare chest. Her skin, unlike so many of the other dancers, was creamy and smooth. Pamela had once said she didn't go in for tans.

"You shouldn't be here, baby." Pamela pulled up the chair next to Tony's.

"We need to talk," said Kozol. "Razner's dead."

"I know," said Pamela. She'd nuzzled up close and whispered in Tony's ear.

He was very much aware of her bare shoulder touching

his and the soft curve of her warm breast nonchalantly pressing against his arm through the fabric of his suit.

"I heard it on the news," whispered the dancer.

"It was on the news?"

"Yes. I saw it on the television in the office. Your name was mentioned."

"I didn't kill him—"

"And the police have been here talking to everybody. They were looking for me."

"What did you tell them?"

She shrugged. "Nothing. I wasn't even here. My shift only started an hour ago. You're in big trouble, baby."

"But I didn't kill him!"

"You better hope you didn't, Tony. If Michael's partners or one of the boys think you did, you're a dead man."

"I had nothing to do with it, damn it. And you know it."

The dancer on stage left to a smattering of applause. She cruised between the tables exchanging feels for dollar bills. Another girl took her place on stage and the show went on.

"Damn it, Pamela," said Kozol, a touch of sadness in his voice, "why did you set me up?"

Pamela sighed and reached for Tony's hand under the table. "I'm sorry, Tony. Razner would've killed me if I hadn't. I've got a little boy. He's only six years old, remember? I was afraid."

"Did you kill Razner?"

"Me? Last time I saw Michael was here at the club on Thursday night. And he was plenty lively then. Why? Do

I look like a killer to you?" laughed Pamela.

"Not in that outfit."

"Look, guys like Razner, they have no real friends and lots of enemies, you know. Anybody could have done him."

"Yeah, but they left the body in my uncle's restaurant and the police would like to put my head on a platter for the D.A."

"You sure you didn't do it? Maybe I could be your alibi, sort of make up for what I did to you."

Kozol didn't bother to answer. There wasn't much a person could do to make up for ruining one's reputation and career all in one fell swoop. "Isn't there anything at all that you can think of that might help?"

Pamela shook her head. "Sorry. Damn, Mitch is looking this way."

Tony flinched. Mitch, a six foot-four muscle with a bristle brush hair cut and absolutely no sense of humor was one of Razner's boys. And like all good boys, he did what Razner told him, no questions asked.

Kozol wondered who Mitch would adopt for his next master, because men such as Mitch were like dogs and functioned best when someone more imperial barked the orders and held the leash.

Pamela put her arms around Tony and jumped in his lap. "Ouch!" she said with surprise. "You must not be as angry with me as you say, baby!"

"What are you doing?" demanded Kozol.

"Lap dancing. Now shut up and enjoy it. And don't look to your right. If Mitch spots us, he'll kill you. So be quiet and play along. And put your arms around me, stupid."

Tony felt himself getting dizzy. But he knew better, or thought he did, than to get involved with a stripper again, especially one who'd been sleeping with a reported mobster, a mobster who had set him up to be disbarred and who Kozol was himself now accused of murdering in revenge. "I've got to go," he said, attempting to rise.

"Okay," consented Pamela, her eyes scanning the room. "It looks like Mitch is gone. Listen," she said, as Tony turned to go, "if you really didn't kill Michael and want to know who did maybe you should ask his wife."

"Laura?"

"She knew all about me and Michael. Hell hath no fury like a woman scorned, right?"

"Why would she talk to me?"

"I didn't say she would. Michael's funeral is in two days at All Saints."

"The big church by the beach?"

"That's right. There's going to be a wake afterwards at his house. Everyone's been invited. Just crash it. Even Mitch wouldn't dare to mess with you there."

Kozol nodded and headed for the exit.

"Call me!" shouted Pamela.

FOUR

The pillow was twisted like a torus under his neck and his neck was stiff as cheap leather. Tony opened his eyes and moaned.

The telephone on the nightstand was off the hook. Kozol had pulled the receiver from the cradle in desperation the night before when he'd come home after what seemed like a wasted trip to Girls Galore and found his answering machine tape full of calls about the murder.

The phone had been ringing wildly even as he'd turned his key in the lock last night. Between the media and the crackpots, Tony had been deluged with questions and insults. In short order, Kozol had decided to disconnect from the world.

Now it was morning.

He'd have to open the damn restaurant.

Why? He didn't know. It wasn't like there were going to be any customers now, after the murder had made all the papers and television. Though Tony wasn't so sure business had been so good before the murder either. Maybe that girl, what was her name? Nina. Perhaps she could straighten out the books. She seemed to understand bookkeeping well enough. Give him some idea where he stood.

If only he'd been lucky enough to have inherited a fortune like Uncle Jonathan, he'd be able to live a life of easy pleasures. Forget about being a failed lawyer, forget about Dairy Delites. Disconnect entirely.

Kozol crawled out of bed and started the coffee. The kitchen was a mess. He found a sort of clean mug and gave it a cursory rinse under the cold water. It could dry while he took a hot shower.

Tony started toward the bedroom, then turned and went back to the kitchen. On second thought, since he was going to take a shower anyway, he'd might as well take the coffee mug with him and give it a good hot wash as well.

For good measure, Kozol grabbed a small plate and some silverware from the pile which had begun growing in the sink and since spread to the counter. Somehow he had never gotten around to using the dishwasher.

Kozol gave himself a mental pat on the back. He should have thought of this long ago.

He set his breakfast ware down on the bedspread and gingerly set the telephone receiver back in its cradle. Connected to the real world once again.

As soon as Tony did so, the phone burst out shrilly, ringing seemingly louder than ever before, as if angry at being forced to hold its breath for so long. Kozol quickly picked up the receiver and dropped it to the carpeted floor with a bang and headed for his shower cum dishwasher. Disconnected once more.

He closed his eyes and let the warm water massage his back. It was a nearly religious experience. Life had its moments.

There was a frightening sound of splintering wood. Tony dropped his favorite coffee mug to the blue-tiled floor of his Roman-style shower. The cup burst into dozens of sharp fragments. Make that ex-favorite coffee mug.

The sharp ceramic bits cut his toes as he slipped and struggled to turn off the water as Officer Keyes and two clean cut officers in sharp blue suits burst into the bathroom with their guns drawn.

"Yaugh!" screamed Kozol in pain and fear, as the three officers burst into the shower with guns aiming menacingly at parts both public and private. He recognized Keyes instantly, almost.

Blood ran from Tony's toes, mixing with the warm shower water and making its way down the drain. "What the hell are you doing here?"

Officer Keyes dropped his gun. "We got a call saying you might be in trouble or even dead. Check the place out," Officer Keyes said to the other officers.

One, Kozol noticed on clearer more painful inspection, was a woman. "Well, I'm fine," he answered with a nervous and embarrassed tremor.

"There was no answer to your doorbell, not even when I knocked."

"The doorbell's been busted for a month," said Tony,

beginning to shiver from the cold. "And I didn't hear you knocking. What did you do, bust down the door?"

"Had to. Like I said, we got a call from someone who was concerned about your safety."

"From who?"

"Leilah Richards."

"Huh?"

"She works for you."

"Oh, that Leilah. Do you mind putting that thing away," Tony said, pointing to Officer Keyes weapon, "and handing me that towel?"

Officer Keyes holstered his nine millimeter and tossed Kozol a dry bath towel. "You're bleeding."

Tony wrapped the towel snugly around his waist. His wet hair dripped into his eyes. He rubbed it away. "I cut my feet when you burst in here like that. What do you expect?"

Officer Keyes studied the tile floor of the shower. "A coffee cup?"

Kozol scowled and said nothing in reply. Officer Keyes didn't seem ready for the shower cum dishwasher concept just yet. Maybe he was married and had a wife to do the little things for him. Too bad. He wouldn't appreciate the concept.

Officer Keyes' two partners returned.

"Coast is clear," said the woman in a firm voice. Her light chestnut hair was tied back tightly in a loose, short ponytail. She had a small but athletic looking body. Her partner looked like he'd been investigating one too many doughnut shop burglaries.

"Why on earth did Leilah think something had

happened to me?"

"Says she tried to call you all morning. First the line was busy all the time and then someone picked up but all she heard was a thud."

Tony groaned and remembered dropping the phone to the floor. He edged his way past Ocean Palm's finest and pulled the phone up by the cord. A tinny sound came from within. "Hello?" he said.

"Mr. Kozol!" shouted Leilah. "Are you all right? Did the police show up? Did somebody try to kill you?" She shot out the questions like rounds from a semi-automatic.

"I'm fine. I dropped the phone, that's all."

"Ohmygod, you mean you're really all right?"

"Yes, I'm really all right. Well, except for that moment there when the police crashed through my front door and found me standing naked in the shower and I thought I might die from embarrassment," he said with a thick slice of sarcasm.

"Oh, jeez, sorry, boss."

Tony sighed. "That's okay. But what on earth possessed you to call the police?"

"Well," she answered, sounding short of breath, "you were supposed to be here to take inventory like you said and you didn't show up and me and Joe kept calling and you didn't answer and we started thinking and got worried. After all, there's already been one guy killed and then I tried calling again and somebody picked up and all I heard was that thud and I thought maybe the killer had got you too!"

Kozol could hear her gasping for a breath.

"So, I dialed the police on the other line."

STIFF IN THE FREEZER

"Well, thanks for caring. At least it sounds like you don't think I killed Razner," Tony said this loudly for Officer Keyes and the others benefit.

"Who knows?" replied Leilah. "Maybe you offed Razner and now somebody's trying to do you. Are you coming in for inventory or what? The place is kind of a mess now that the police have been through it. They aren't the neatest bunch in the world. Gloria and Amelia are helping clean up."

"Yes, well, I appreciate that," said Tony, grateful that for the police this was a one-sided conversation. "I'll be in soon."

"Guess we'll be going now," said Officer Keyes. He made a note in his pad. The others were already in the outside corridor.

Kozol noticed Mrs. Pikipsky sneaking a look through a crack in her door.

"Hey, what about my door?" Tony shouted. The apartment door leaned inward and looked as forlorn as a broken gull's wing. The hinges had been ripped from the wall. The frame was splintered from the force of the lock being broken.

Officer Keyes stopped and turned. "Yeah, I'd get that fixed if I were you."

Kozol kicked the doorjamb and screamed. "Damn," he hissed, grabbing his twice abused feet. Tony made his way back across the plush white carpet to his bedroom where he hoped to find something to bandage his wounds and then dress.

It wasn't hard to find his way, he only had to follow the fresh bloody footprints.

Before leaving for the restaurant Kozol telephoned the building superintendent and left a message on his machine asking him to fix the front door.

Tony propped up the busted front door as best he could.

¤

"Grab an apron!" Leilah ran past Tony carrying a tray of burger rolls.

"It's about time you got here," muttered Joe, dripping sweat which rolled off his forehead and sizzled in the flames of the grill. He flipped burgers expertly up and down the grates. "Come on, get some buns going!"

Kozol made a note to himself to require the help to wear hats as a sanitation measure, and tossed several open buns on the stainless steel counter. He gave each bottom a squirt of ketchup. "What's going on? There must be close to a hundred people in here." If the burger business was this good his financial troubles could be over, he realized.

"Beats me," said Joe. "I've never seen it so crowded on a Sunday."

"Got two jumbo meal packs. Where's the drinks?" Leilah shouted from the register.

"Hey, is that him?" Tony heard a man in line ask.

"Yeah, that's him," answered Leilah. She sounded tired.

Nina ran over with two sodas and bagged them.

"You were supposed to be working on the books," Kozol said.

Nina shrugged. "Leilah said she needed me down here. I don't mind."

Tony looked at the line of customers. The parking lot was full. There must have been thirty or forty people waiting at the window.

"Come on, boss," said Joe, "box 'em up and move them down the line. Danny's waiting."

"Who's Danny?"

"The french fry guy!"

"Oh, right," Kozol replied. He stuffed the burgers none too gingerly into their boxes and Danny tossed in the fries and closed them up. Nina took the order to the pickup window, added the drinks, collected the customer's ticket and the whole thing started all over again.

Gloria and Amelia took care of the customers on the ice cream side.

"Damn," said Tony, when the crowd had faded, "I'm exhausted." He leaned against the ice cream machine which swirled behind him. The inherent coolness soothed his aching back. His lacerated toes pounded like relentless demons at the Gates of Hell.

Nina handed him a lime freeze.

"Thanks."

"You look like hell, boss," said Joe.

"I told you not to wear those suits," complained Leilah.

Kozol glanced down. Another four hundred dollar suit ruined. He made another mental note—no more suits and bigger aprons.

"So," said Tony, "is it always like this?"

"No, they just wanted to see you." Leilah grabbed a fry

from the warmer and rolled it over her lips once before inhaling. She squatted on the floor Indian style.

"Me? You mean because I'm the new owner? Of course. I'm flattered."

Leilah laughed. "Save it," she answered bluntly. "They all think you killed Razner and want to get a look at you."

"What—"

"People are ghouls, Mr. Kozol," replied Leilah. She rose and straightened her apron. "At least business is good, consider yourself lucky."

"Yeah, lucky," echoed Joe. "You got anyone else you can kill? Maybe we could all get raises!" His high pitched laugh rebounded off the walls.

Tony supposed he should be grateful. He'd been afraid the murder would kill his fledgling enterprise and instead business was booming because of it.

"Hey, who's in charge here?"

Kozol turned his attention to the order window. "Can I help you?"

"Yeah," replied the stranger with a tone of annoyance. He wore a blue wind breaker and a Marlins baseball cap. His face was as mottled as the Sea of Rains.

"Well?" said Tony, impatiently.

"Well, it stinks out there, that's what."

"What are you talking about?" Kozol leaned forward and sniffed the air. It was burgers and grease, vanilla and chili.

"Not here, outside. It stinks outside."

"What are you telling me for?"

"It's your restaurant, isn't it?"

"That's right. But it's not my goddamn planet!"

Tony felt a hundred eyes focus in on him like tiny satellite radar. His face grew warm.

The man in the baseball cap stepped back and threw up his hands.

It was like a scene from a bad movie, thought Kozol, a hopeless situation.

"I try to give you some advice—some information for your own good and this is how you talk to me, a paying customer? I'm never eating here again!" the man shouted, at what had to be close to the topmost power of his lungs and tossed the remains of a burger to the floor.

The incensed, now ex-customer stormed out the door, turned, gesticulated vaguely in the direction of the charity clothing drop-off bin and shouted something which Tony was relieved he couldn't hear.

In return, Kozol grinned tauntingly and pinched his nose for the man's benefit. The man in the cap shot him the finger and jumped into his car.

"Idiot," muttered Tony.

"Good management skills," said Joe.

"Yep, the boss is MBA material all right," replied Leilah, matter-of-factly.

FIVE

Black limousines studded the half-circle drive like jewels on a necklace. Up and down both sides of the street more cars spilled over. It seemed Michael Razner had had lots of friends, or associates, anyhow, realized Kozol. Come to pay their last respects or to make sure the bastard really leaves?

Kozol parked his aging Saab on the grass between the mailbox and a small oak. Tony was proud of the old car. Through various owners it had successfully, if not swiftly, rolled along for over one hundred and fifty-seven thousand miles. They don't get much sturdier than that.

Of course, the window on the passenger's side had gotten stuck in the down position some weeks ago. But that was no big thing. Kozol would get it repaired as soon as he got some money together.

Tony checked out his reflection in the driver's side window and wondered one last time what he was doing there at Razner's house. His reflection provided no answers.

A middle-aged woman in a navy blue suit was heading for the open front door. Kozol stepped in behind her. He was now in enemy territory and felt that all eyes were on him like rifle barrels.

A sharp crack of laughter broke out to Tony's right. He flinched.

The high-ceiling entryway opened up onto the living room which in turn looked out on the pool deck and the wide intracoastal waterway. There was a bar set up between the sliding glass doors and the swimming pool.

Kozol judged there to be at least seventy-five people present. The majority were outside the house, standing around the pool, drinks in hand. With the cool breeze coming in off the Atlantic and few clouds in the sky it was a perfect day for a funeral or a party. Tony wondered which this was.

No doubt about it, Michael Razner had enjoyed the good life. The Razner home was situated on the fairest street along the intracoastal waterway in Ocean Palm. It was also one of the largest homes on the block with a four car garage and, Kozol guessed, about twenty rooms and a boat dock where Razner's 60 ft Chris-Craft was tied down.

The yacht was one of Razner's prized toys. Tony had been on the boat once before when Razner took him from Pompano to Fort Lauderdale where they'd had lunch at one of the expensive intracoastal restaurants that catered to the boating crowd.

The house smelled of expensive perfume and fresh-cut

flowers. Kozol couldn't hide his surprise when he spotted Pamela chatting with a somber looking, middle-aged couple on one of the black leather sofas. She had a lot of nerve.

Tony was wondering whether he should go over and talk to her when he felt a tug on his sleeve and turned guiltily, half expecting a punch in his face. It was only a waiter. Kozol waved him off.

A face he recognized came his way.

"Tony, imagine seeing you here."

"Hello, Richard." Kozol managed a smile he didn't feel. Richard Tishman was one of the last people he felt like seeing. They'd been friends in law school. Since then, Tishman was on the fast track to partnership with Brownstone and Leland, one of the largest law firms in south Florida.

Tony had done some work for them on the side. He'd been painfully aware that Richard was tossing him bones, but when you're hungry you have no choice. You eat bones. When Razner had gone to the State Bar and accused Kozol of money laundering, Tishman, like all his uppity colleagues, had frozen him out.

"I'm kind of surprised to see you here." Tishman adjusted his tie. The exercise probably represented as much physical exercise as the man had ever done. His fine fingers appeared baby soft and uncalloused.

The whole damn suit had to cost a thousand bucks, thought Tony, sourly. "Yeah, well, the same goes for you. What did you have to do with Razner?"

"Brownstone and Leland represent him now, that is, his estate. His wife is usually such a cool bird. She's been bawling her eyes out since finding out about her husband though. Did she invite you?"

"Not exactly. I wanted to nose around."

"A nose could get cut off in a place like this, Tony. Listen, you're my friend, if you need some help, a good attorney—"

"I didn't murder anybody! I don't need an attorney."

"Hey–hey, lighten up," said Richard. "This is no time nor place to create a scene, buddy." He put a cool hand on Kozol's shoulder and pulled him closer.

Tishman's breath smelled of peppermint candies.

"I didn't mean anything. I'm sorry about your practice. But you've got to admit, it's your own fault for screwing around with a mob boss's girl."

Richard took a swig of champagne and laughed. "I'll bet it was almost worth it, though, a bitch like that—"

"Shut up, Richard, will you?"

"What are you mad at me for? Believe me, I did everything I could to persuade the Florida Bar otherwise—"

"Yes, I'll bet you did."

"Of course, now, with Razner dead maybe the Bar will see things differently. If you did kill him and can get away with it you just might be able to tack that old law degree up on the wall again."

Tony was just about to tack his fist to Richard's all too perfect white teeth when Laura Razner suddenly appeared between the two of them.

"Mr. Kozol," she said, taking Tony's hand in hers. Her face looked slightly puffy. Stress lines appeared at the corners of her hazel-colored eyes. Razner's wife.

Kozol had rarely seen her in the past. She wore a clingy black dress that fell to just below the knee accented with diamond earrings and a glistening diamond necklace. Even her watch looked as if someone had raided a small diamond mine just to craft it. Except for twenty extra pounds or so she still managed to look quite pretty. But then Ocean Palm society demanded that of its elite.

Tony could tell she had been drinking. Plenty. She wobbled slightly, off balance. Her eyes were bloodshot. Was it the tears or the alcohol, he wondered.

"So good of you to come. Michael thought highly of you. He said what a good attorney you are."

"Was," replied Kozol. Her hand felt warm in his and she still hadn't let go.

"Do you mind, Richard?"

"Certainly not." Richard nodded and departed.

"You have a lovely home," said Tony, being more polite than he felt.

"Thank you, Mr. Kozol. I'm quite proud of my home. I love this place very much. A lot of work went into building and decorating. I wouldn't trade it for anything. My poor Michael worked so hard to build it for me."

"Your husband cost me my career."

Laura Razner shrugged and a look of sadness passed over her face. "Michael wasn't perfect."

Tony thought Mrs. Razner had glanced over at Pamela as she spoke, but he couldn't be certain.

"I noticed you at the funeral, I believe."

"Yes, I was there." Kozol had attended the funeral service from a distance. At the funeral home he had come in late and sat in the back, looking over the gathered crowd for suspects, like they did in the movies. He wondered which one of the bereaved, if any, had had the guts to kill Razner.

Detective Fender had been there along with Officer Keyes, apparently they'd had the same idea. Or perhaps they were there keeping an eye on his own movements. A fast talking New Yorker whose neck barely fit in his collar gave the eulogy.

Tony had followed the funeral procession to the cemetery and watched from afar. Kozol had squirmed throughout the burial service. When he got back to his car Fender and Keyes had been waiting for him.

"So why does a man attend the funeral of the person who supposedly framed him?" said Fender loudly.

"Do you mind not leaning on the car," replied Tony.

"Come to make sure you did the job right?" Fender answered his own question without moving.

"I'd like to go if you don't mind."

"It would be best for you to limit your movements, Mr. Kozol," said Officer Keyes. "Razner's family might find your presence here quite disconcerting."

"You trying to intimidate someone?" asked Detective Fender. "That's obstruction of justice."

"Obstruct this—" said Tony, saluting the officer with his finger.

"Listen, wise ass," said Fender, "you don't make a move in this town we don't know about and don't you forget it."

"I'll keep it in mind," said Kozol. Detective Fender stepped away from the car just in the nick of time as Tony sped off.

Fortunately neither that oaf Fender or his partner, Officer Keyes, seemed to have invited themselves to the Razner house.

"Come," Mrs. Razner said, leading Kozol by the hand. They went outside toward the bar. Her hair smelled of roses, her breath of white wine. Mitch stepped in their path.

"What's he doing here?" Mitch demanded ominously. He wore the same dark suit that he always wore. His bear sized hand reached out in Tony's direction.

"That's enough, Mitch," said Mrs. Razner. "Mr. Kozol has come to pay his respects."

"But he's the one who—"

"That's enough, Mitch. Nothing must spoil this day. Now, be a dear," she said, "and check the grounds, will you?"

Mitch exhaled through his nostrils like a caged bull, nodded and stalked away.

Tony wondered if perhaps Mrs. Razner herself might be strong-willed enough to adopt the overgrown puppy.

Laura Razner handed Kozol a glass of white wine, tapped his glass to her own and said, "The question does bear asking, does it not? Why are you here, Mr. Kozol?"

"Looking for Michael's killer," Tony said bluntly, deciding on the direct approach.

Laura let out a polite little laugh. "There are some, Mitch included, as you saw, who would say the killer was you, Mr. Kozol."

"They'd be wrong," replied Tony. "I didn't kill him."

"Then who did?"

"You don't seem too upset, if you don't mind my

saying so," Kozol said. He realized he was treading on dangerous ground now.

"I loved my husband, Mr. Kozol. I met Michael when I was sixteen years old, a mere girl. I didn't know what I wanted and then Michael came into my life. He was three years older than me and so ambitious. I used to get dizzy just listening to him talk about all the things he planned to do.

And he gave me all this," she said raising her glass and gesturing toward the house and grounds. "We were together for thirty-four years and he gave me everything."

Tony sensed the melancholy in her voice. "No one is perfect, Mrs. Razner. Were you aware of your husband's—" Kozol hesitated over the correct phrasing, "indiscretions?"

Mrs. Razner's face seemed to darken. "I believe you should leave now, Mr. Kozol."

"But don't you want to know who killed your husband?"

"I see Mitch has completed his rounds," said Mrs. Razner. "I must insist that you go."

"But if we could just talk about what Michael was involved in, maybe we could—"

"Good afternoon," said Laura. She leaned forward, one hand on Tony's shoulder and whispered in his ear. "Let it go," she said.

Was that her tongue licking his ear? Kozol sighted an unhappy looking Mitch heading back in their direction. Tony broke loose and made for the door.

SIX

Tony ran for his car with the Hound of the Baskervilles on his tail, or so it felt. Pamela was waiting for him, leaning with her elbows propped back against the forest green hood of his run down old Saab. Looking a damn sight better than a woman ought to in a dark blue mourning dress.

"Hi," she said. "How'd you make out in there?"

"Not so good. I don't think she likes me."

Pamela laughed. "You mean Laura?"

"Yeah. She does seem pretty broken up about her husband, however."

"Mrs. Razner was devoted to that guy. It's amazing. You know, she cooked his breakfast and dinner personally every day. Poor woman, I think her whole world revolved around the bastard."

"And you?"

"Me what? Oh, you mean me and Michael. I told

you," she said, a trace of hardness betraying her masked face, "it was an arrangement."

"Right," said Kozol, making the one word sound like a twenty page indictment.

"Listen mister big shot, what the hell do you know?" shouted Pamela. She shoved Tony backwards with her hands and pounded on his chest. "Just because you went to college and became a big shot lawyer you think you have a right to judge me?"

"I—"

"Well, you don't. Did I ever tell you my dad ran off when I was three, that my mom was an alcoholic who barely came home? And even when she did she was never really there, if you know what I mean. Wasted, completely wasted. So I made some mistakes too. But I'm raising my son and doing what I have to. That's survival. That's what I do!"

Pamela's hardness surprised him.

"Maybe if you'd chosen another road to survival you'd have some respect for yourself. That's why you're angry and yelling at me, because you have no self pride!" Tony shot back angrily.

"Oh, now he's Mister Psychology. What is it, Tony, you minor in psychology at college?" She kicked the car door leaving a pointed indent from the toe of her high heel shoe.

"Hey!"

Pamela turned to leave. She was taunting him. Kozol was in no mood. He swung her around. But before he could think of something to say she spoke first.

"Asshole," she said.

Tony let her go. His arms dropped to his side as he went rigid with rage. His hands clenched and unclenched as he fought to control himself.

Without further words he went to his car and yanked on the handle so hard that the car gave a sideways lurch. The front driver's side tire caught his eye. Flat.

"Shit!" he screamed. A woman in a black and white jogging suit walking a pair of leashed dalmatians glared at him from across the street. The dogs looked mean and underfed and so he wisely ignored her.

"What's wrong?" Pamela moved over to Tony's side of the car.

"I've got a goddamn flat tire," said Kozol, suddenly feeling as deflated as the old Michelin. "It just keeps getting worse." He stuck his hands in his pockets and leaned his forehead against the top of the lame automobile. "Summertime. Florida. Dark green car. Hot," he said.

Pamela laughed. "Come on," she said, pulling Tony's head from the heat, "you'll hurt yourself." Pamela took Kozol's hand. "Let's go. I'll give you a lift."

"What about my car?"

"It'll be fine here. Though I hope Mrs. Razner doesn't realize it's you parking on her lawn. But never mind. I've got a friend with a tow truck. He'll take care of it."

Tony acceded and climbed in the passenger's side.

"Where to?" said Pamela. She drove a black Camaro. It looked and smelled brand new.

"Nice car."

"Don't start—" warned Pamela.

"Okay, okay. I only meant nice car." They passed the

guard shack and swung out onto Federal Highway. "You could drop me off at the restaurant if you don't mind driving down to Ocean Palm."

"No problem. So, you wanna tell me about it?"

Kozol described the last several days of his life to Pamela. He explained how his uncle had inherited an estate from an aunt in Michigan and left Tony the restaurant, out of pity he supposed, since Kozol's life was in such a shambles.

He told her how Razner's body had been found in the freezer and how the police seemed intent on fingering him for the murder. She seemed to pay close attention, nodding in all the right places and asking specific questions.

"Who do you think killed him then?" asked Pamela.

Tony shrugged and rubbed his forehead. It still stung. And it was no magic lamp. No good answers were forthcoming. "Mrs. Razner? A hit man? I don't know. And frankly I wouldn't care except that it happened at Dairy Delites and I'm the number one suspect."

"You don't have any other ideas about who killed him? Any hunches?"

Tony shook his head no.

"What about the police?" pressed Pamela. "Have they found anything? I mean, maybe there are some clues that could lead them to the real killer and clear you, Tony."

"No, nothing. In fact, they don't even seem interested in trying to find anyone else. They seem so sure I did it that they're only looking for pieces of the puzzle that add up to one thing—me."

Pamela patted Kozol's leg.

"It's incredible," Tony went on, "first Razner screws

up my life while he's alive and then he drives the screws in even deeper after he's dead and gone to hell."

"Poor Michael, though," said Pamela. The look on Kozol's face was one of incredulity. Pamela seemed to ignore it.

"I think he was getting tired of the business," she explained. "Plus the government's been hounding him. Even though you got him out of that last scrape, everybody from the IRS to the Feds to the State up until his death were trying to get something on him."

"Take a left."

"He used to call them the government bulldogs. He couldn't understand why they wouldn't leave him in peace. And as tough a guy as Michael Razner was, he was scared to death of going to jail. Said they'd never put him there."

"Yeah, well, I can't say I share any sentiment for Razner. Who gets everything now that he's gone?"

Pamela swerved to avoid an elderly woman in an ancient Crown Victoria who drifted between two lanes. The old woman's head was barely even with the dashboard. This was just another of Florida's road hazards, like the potholes and possums.

"I don't know precisely. Michael had some partners in the club and a couple of other businesses he owned. Other than that, I expect Laura gets it all."

"Plenty for everybody. Mrs. Razner won't have to worry about flipping burgers."

"I don't know what he'll do with his place in Jamaica."

"He's got another place?"

"Yeah, a house on the beach that he bought about a

month or two ago. He was excited about it. I remember when he closed the deal—told us all about it. Between you and me," she said, in false confidence, "he had a girlfriend there. So maybe he left the house to her, who knows—" she said nonchalantly.

"Another girlfriend?" Christ, thought Kozol. How did he do it? "What was her name? Maybe she knows something about all of this."

"Sorry, baby. I don't have a clue. Michael was a pretty discreet man. I'm not even sure his wife knew about the house. The nature of the business and all. He'd go to Jamaica for a few days at a time and come back with some sun on his back and a big grin on his face."

"Meaning?"

"I know that grin," Pamela said, knowledgeably.

Tony felt disgusted. "If you come up with her name, let me know," he said. Kozol stepped out of the car and shut the door.

"So, this is it, huh?" The Dairy Delites parking lot had about six cars scattered about.

"Yeah, impressive, isn't it?" Tony spotted Joe leaning over the counter next to the register with his eyes half shut.

"Baby, it's not so bad. You mind if I drop by and try it sometime?" Her deep green eyes pulled him in.

"No, I don't mind."

¤

Kozol gave Joe a rap on the forehead. "Wake up!"

"Oh, sorry, boss," Joe said drowsily. "Guess I dosed off

there for a sec—"

"Where are all the customers?" asked Tony, looking around in desperation. The other day the seats had been packed and now they were nearly empty. A pair of amorous teenagers were hanging out in the far corner. A family of four were consuming matching burgers. Another man sat alone, sifting through the remains of a hot fudge brownie sundae. Kozol wondered if he'd even make enough to cover the day's payroll.

"The circus has moved on," answered Leilah, popping up from behind the ice machine. Her hands were smudged with grease.

"What do you mean the circus has moved on?"

"I mean the press and the sickos are off looking for the next show. You're old news. Until, I mean, unless you get busted."

"What's wrong with the ice machine?" Tony asked, ignoring bad thoughts of his future. He watched Gloria polishing the chrome blenders with a towel. Maybe, he hoped in desperation, a genie would appear from the blender if she rubbed hard enough and put him out of his increasing misery.

"Nothing much," Leilah said with a shrug. "Hose was leaking, I fixed it. By the way, Nina's been carrying on like a caged hen."

"What's her problem?" asked Kozol, wearily. Running a restaurant was one thing but having to deal with all the different personalities was quickly becoming too much for him to deal with.

"She's looking for you. Complaining about what a mess you're in financially—"

Tony cut her off in a loud voice. "Mess I'm in financially? That's the least of my worries! In case any of you have forgotten," he said, for the benefit of all the employees in range, "I've got a lot bigger mess to deal with. That stupid son of a bitch, Razner, ruined my life!"

The look on Leilah's face went from startled to stony. Joe began twitching his eyebrows.

"None of this would be happening to me if it wasn't for him. At least he's dead and that's about the only good thing I can say about him."

"Mister Kozol—" said Gloria.

"What?" said Tony rudely, his pulse racing like an Indy car.

Gloria gestured with her head.

"What?" he repeated in exasperation. She gestured again and Kozol got it. He turned and found himself nose to nose with Detective Fender.

"God," said Fender with a smirk. Officer Keyes stood beside him, poker-faced. "You make this so easy."

Tony's face was redder than the artificially colored cherry topping they served to the customers. "Don't sneak up on me like that!"

Fender never stopped smiling. "We walked right in the front door. Maybe you should put a bell on that thing." Fender's breath smelled of cigarettes.

Kozol stepped back out of range.

"Go ahead, continue, Mister Kozol. You were telling us how glad you are that Michael Razner is dead—"

"I've got nothing to say."

Fender stuck out his hand and Officer Keyes placed a photocopied document in his palm. "Let's talk about this then," he said with apparent relish. "Care to explain where a debarred attorney comes up with a fifty thousand dollar deposit?" He held the bank records up within inches of Tony's nose.

Joe whistled. "Wow, you're rich, boss."

"Be quiet, Joe!" Kozol turned back to Fender and Keyes. "Listen," he tried to explain, "I don't know what this is all about. I don't have fifty thousand dollars. I don't have a thousand dollars. It's got to be a mistake!"

"Fifty thousand dollars?" Nina had appeared out of nowhere. "Hey, you could really straighten out the restaurant with that kind of money. Pay off the debts. Maybe think about remodeling and updating some of the older equipment. That'd be a good down payment. You could amortize the rest of the cost over—"

"Shut up!" Tony cried, more out of fear than anger, but the damage was done.

Nina covered her face and ran toward the backroom in tears.

"Quite a way you've got with the ladies there, Mister Kozol," taunted Fender.

If Fender hadn't been a police officer, Tony would have slugged him.

"Guess that will be all for now. Come on, Keyes." Fender rolled up the photocopied bank records of Kozol's personal checking account like a flute and stuck it to his fat lips. "Hear that?" he said, after miming the movements of a flautist, blowing through the paper and moving his fingers in an annoyingly childish fashion.

"Hear what?" demanded Tony.

"Music to my ears," chided Fender. "Everything you

say is music to my ears."

Kozol glowered but held his tongue.

Officer Keyes held the door as Detective Fender went past him. "Better have somebody empty these trash barrels out here. It stinks."

"Yeah, everybody keeps saying that," Joe said.

Tony turned his evil glare to Joe.

"Well," said Joe, squirming, "they do."

SEVEN

"**W**here's Nina?" asked Kozol. The backroom was empty save for Amelia who sat reading her Cosmo. There was a peeled, half-sliced onion on the cutting tray by her side.

"She's gone," replied Amelia.

Flip.

She turned the page slowly.

"Gone? Where did she go?"

Amelia almost looked up from her study of an ad for glossy lipsticks. "How should I know? She came running back here shaking like a tree in a thunderstorm and crying her heart out. Other than that she didn't say a word."

"Haven't you got any work to do?"

"I'm on break," answered Amelia with a huff. "You ever try slicing a tray of onions and lettuce with a blunted knife?"

"Where's the good one?"

"Who knows? Things have a way of disappearing around here. Better order another one."

"Fine, tell Leilah," replied Tony, not in the least bit interested in stupid cutlery details.

"By the way, some customer was complaining about the smell. He said—"

Kozol turned livid. He reached under the sink, grabbed a fresh can of Lysol disinfectant and sprayed the air overhead. "There. Is that better?"

"Hey, watch it!" shouted Amelia, covering her hair. "Geez, that stuff makes me nauseous."

Tony went out to the dining room, shaking and spraying, shaking and spraying. Outside, he sprayed the trash cans, the parking spaces, the doors, the charity drop-off and for good measure the hibiscus that grew alongside the building. Out of Lysol, he tossed the can in the nearest bin.

"Does anybody know where Nina lives?" Kozol demanded.

"Over near the elementary school, I think," said Gloria. "She mentioned living in an apartment complex next door to it, if I remember correctly."

"Do you know the name of the place?"

"No."

"Her address is on the card I had her fill out," said Leilah.

"Great," said Tony. He rifled through the file box on top the icemaker in the backroom and took out the card with Nina's name and address written in sharp, clear print. He stuffed the card in his trousers.

"What do you want that for?" asked Leilah.

"I feel bad about what happened—I should apologize."

"Apologize! What about me?" said Joe.

"What about you?" shot back Kozol.

"Nothing." Joe grabbed the damp towel that seemed always to hang from his black leather belt, turned and wiped at the wall.

"Can I borrow somebody's car?" Tony asked.

"Rode my bike," said Joe. "Always ride it when the weather's nice." He mumbled without turning around.

"What happened to your car?" Leilah asked.

"Flat tire."

"You can borrow mine, I suppose," said Leilah with obvious hesitation. "Just so long as you take care of it and if Gloria can give me a ride home if you're not back when I leave, Mr. Kozol."

"Sure," said Gloria. "Mike's picking me up. He won't mind."

"Great," said Tony. He held out his hand. Leilah grabbed her purse off the shelf and fished out the keys. Her keys were on a Snoopy key ring. Joe Cool with sunglasses.

"Come on, I'll show you which one." Leilah led Kozol out to a sun worn, red Jeep Cherokee with balding tires.

Tony unlocked the driver's side door and opened it. An uncapped lipstick, a small notebook and a paperback novel fell to the pavement.

"Watch it," said Leilah, picking up her belongings.

"Sorry," said Kozol. "But you've got enough junk in here."

"It's just the way I like it." Leilah tossed the lipstick, novel and notebook over the backseat. "Be careful."

STIFF IN THE FREEZER

Tony nodded and headed off.

The Meadows Apartments where Nina resided was a two building, two storied complex painted mint green, a horrid shade that the city fathers should have outlawed. The double buildings hugged the roads at the intersection of Sixth Street and Anderton Road, beside which was Ocean Palm Elementary School.

A few teens shot hoops in the open playground. Tony parked the Cherokee in a space reserved for guests and wandered toward the pool where several ladies sat like oiled peanuts, slowly roasting in the overbearing Florida sun.

One girl was reading a college psych textbook. She wore a red bikini. The bandages on Tony's toes were bigger. If she had wanted to, she could have gotten a job at Girls Galore.

Kozol stopped at her feet and spoke. "Hi."

A rivulet of beaded sweat ran down her taut, cocoa colored belly to her crotch. Other than the slow rise and fall of her chest, the girl didn't move.

Didn't respond.

"Excuse me," said Tony. "I'm looking for a woman named Nina. Nina Lasher. Do you know her?"

The pretty girl looked at Kozol over the top of her sunglasses. Her straight blond hair was tucked behind her head in a loose ponytail. "Sorry, 'fraid not."

Tony dug out Nina's file card. "Apartment 204-A."

"Oh, that building over there," pointed the girl, "Upstairs."

"Thanks," said Kozol, trying hard to make eye contact over the top of her glasses. But she had already stuck the book between them. He'd been dismissed.

Tony trotted off to find Nina. There was no elevator. There was an outdoor stairway on each end of the building. Kozol climbed the stairs and knocked on the door. No answer. "Hello!" he called, carefully listening for sounds on the other side.

"What are you doing here?"

Tony whipped around and almost knocked Nina over.

"Ooof!" she cried, struggling to regain her balance and not let go of the two brown paper shopping bags she was carrying.

"Here, let me take those." Kozol grabbed the sacks.

Nina unlocked the door. "So what are you doing here?" she said again, taking back the bags and setting them gently on the kitchen counter. The kitchen was right off the entrance to the left, with beige counters and almond appliances, everything reasonably new and fastidiously clean.

"I came to see you. I didn't think I was going to find you."

"I had to go to the market."

"Listen, about this afternoon—I want to apologize."

Nina placed a bag of oranges in the fruit bin inside the refrigerator and faced him squarely. "Why don't you leave? Don't you have a murder to commit somewhere?"

"Very funny," said Tony. "But this isn't my fault. I mean, I was rude to you and I am sorry. You have to believe that. I'm under a lot of pressure. The police think I killed someone and my uncle's left me a business I know nothing about."

Miss Lasher interrupted him. "I haven't eaten all day

and I am starved. You want something?"

"Well—"

"Fine," said Nina, sternly. She handed Kozol two large white potatoes and a vegetable brush. "Wash these in the sink and I'll see what else I've got."

Nina scampered confidently about the kitchen as she prepared supper, speaking to Tony only when necessary to assign him to some minor task. They ate in the kitchen.

"So what kind of shape am I in?" asked Kozol, scarfing down the last of the potatoes au gratin.

"I'd say there's still time to join a gym."

Tony self-consciously sucked in his gut. "I mean as far as the Dairy Delites goes."

"Oh, it's too early to say for certain, Mister Kozol—"

"Call me Tony."

"Tony," said Nina, as if trying the word on for size, "your uncle was a horrible records keeper. He barely wrote anything down. He still did everything on paper, too. It could take weeks to sift through everything."

Tony frowned.

"You really should update the business by purchasing a decent computer with a bookkeeping and tax program."

"Right, that's a good idea." He'd already realized that whatever money did come in needed to be better accounted for.

"Other than that, it's quite confusing. You seem to have a fair number of customers to support the business and you could always clean the place up a bit and advertise. That would help to increase your customer base. Would you like some more ham?" She held the platter toward him.

"No thanks," replied Kozol, still smarting from her comment about the gym. "I'm busting. Everything was great, though. So what's the problem then besides poor bookkeeping?"

"There isn't any real money. From what I've added up of the invoices your cost of goods is way too high compared to your gross receipts."

"Pardon my French," said Tony. "But what the hell does that mean? I'm a trained attorney not a CPA."

Nina took a sip of herb tea and set the cup down delicately. Steam curled over her fingers. A faint scent of mint rose in the air. "Well, either your uncle was one lousy businessman or—" Her finger followed the curve of her mug.

"Or what?"

Nina's eyes did not meet his.

"Or he was keeping two sets of books."

Kozol didn't need an accounting degree to understand that. "You think he took in a lot more money than he showed?"

"It's possible," answered Nina, with obvious hesitation. "Lots of people do it, I'm sure. Your uncle's taxable income would be substantially less."

Tony gaped. "My Uncle Jonathan? Cheating on his taxes? I don't believe it," he said resolutely. "I mean, you don't know him and Aunt Louise, they're as honest as the Pope and Mother Theresa. There must be some other explanation."

"I'll keep looking if you want." Nina rose and took the plates to the sink.

"Please do."

She rinsed each dish thoroughly and set them side by side in the dishwasher. Kozol helped her carry the rest.

"I've got some leftover pie if you'd like?"

"Well—"

"Come on," said Nina, "I was only joking about the gym before."

"Okay, sure." Still, there was a pretty fair exercise room in his apartment complex, weight machines, treadmills, rowers, the works. Kozol rubbed his belly under the table. He'd have to check it out one of these days.

Nina pulled a foil covered pie pan from the refrigerator and cut them each a slice. "I made it myself."

"It looks great," said Tony. It was apple.

"Let's take it into the living room."

Kozol sat on the dark green sofa. Nina took the matching chair. The room was spartan but cozy. There were a couple of interesting paintings on the wall and one lone eight by ten in a silver frame.

"My parents," stated Nina.

"Oh, do they live nearby?"

"No, Illinois. Daddy has a farm there. I moved to Florida for my job. Maybe I'll move back now. Do you have family in Ocean Palm, Tony? Besides your aunt and uncle, that is."

"No, no one. My parents died when I was in college. Uncle Jonathan and Aunt Louise have always been there for me though. And there's their son, cousin Scott."

"How lucky for you."

"Yes." His fingers scratched at the fabric of the cushions which were soft and smooth. "Once again, I want to apologize about this afternoon, Nina. I shouldn't have snapped at you like that."

"That's all right, Tony. One apology is enough." She rose and went to the kitchen table, returning with their tea. Kozol wasn't much of a tea drinker, but he didn't have the heart to refuse.

"What did the police want anyway?" asked Nina, as she refilled Tony's cup.

"It was about the money. The fifty thousand dollars they said was in my bank account."

"And you don't know how it got there?"

"No!" said Kozol. "Somebody's really setting me up good."

"Was the money deposited as a check or in cash?"

"I don't know," said Tony. "What does that matter?"

"If it was a check it could easily be traced. But if the deposit were cash and somebody dropped it in the night deposit box, well, I don't know if that could be traced back to anyone. You might not be able to prove you were framed but at least we might be able to show that it's possible."

"We?"

"I used to work in a bank, remember? I'll see what I can find out."

"You sound just like Pamela."

"Pamela?"

"Yeah, she was a girlfriend of Razner's."

"Yes, I remember," said Nina, her back stiffening ever so slightly. "She's the one you were running around with. The one who got you in so much trouble."

"Yeah," confessed Kozol. "She was asking me all kinds of questions—the same as you. The problem is that I have no answers."

"When did you see her?"

"At the wake, after the funeral. She was at Razner's house and gave me a ride home. I had a flat tire."

"That's odd."

"What? A flat tire?"

"No," said Nina, shaking her head, "that this girl, Pamela, would be at Michael Razner's home. Doesn't Mrs. Razner know that this girl was—"

"Yeah, she must."

"Really, I can't imagine. I couldn't tolerate it. What sort of things did Pamela want to know?"

"The usual," replied Tony. "Who I thought the murderer might be. What other leads or evidence the police had. That sort of thing. And she told me all about Razner and his girlfriends—"

Tony repeated as much of his conversation with Pamela as he could remember.

"Maybe," suggested Nina, "Pamela is the killer."

"How's that?"

"You mentioned this new girlfriend in Jamaica. Pamela might have felt threatened. Maybe he was growing tired of her. If Razner cut Pamela off financially what would she do? No more cars, no more money. She might have been angry enough to kill him. And she was asking you all kinds of questions about the murder."

"That's true," admitted Kozol. "But it doesn't make her a murderer." Truth was, in spite of his own better judgement Tony was beginning to think he might just pick up where he'd left off with Pamela before Razner had come between them. Maybe he didn't want Pamela to be the murderer.

"It does suggest a motive, though."

"I suppose," Kozol answered halfheartedly.

"You don't sound very interested in finding another suspect. Maybe you really did kill Razner."

"No, no! That's not it. I can't picture Pamela as a cold-blooded killer that's all." Now hot-blooded, that's another thing altogether, Tony mused, lasciviously.

Thoughts he wisely kept to himself.

"You've made a good point. It does sound like enough of a motive to commit murder all right," agreed Kozol, giving the matter some thought. "Yet there's no evidence."

"No, but if you tell this to the police, they'll have to at least consider her a suspect."

Kozol allowed himself his first moment of happiness since his disbarment. "You're right."

EIGHT

There was a knock at the door.

"Who is it?" called Nina through the closed door. She didn't have a peephole.

"Detective Fender, Miss Lasher."

"Geezus, what's he doing here?" cursed Tony in low tones.

Nina shrugged. "I'll have to let him in," she said, almost apologetically.

Kozol stood.

Nina opened the apartment door. "Yes?"

Tony sneaked a look through the pass-through counter between the kitchen and the living room. He could see the ugly, grinning face of Fender as the detective stepped authoritatively into the small entryway, occupying it like so much conquered territory.

Behind him stood Officers Keyes and Murchison, as silent and menacing as the Presidential Guard.

"Is Tony Kozol here, miss?"

"Why yes, he is. What's this all about, detective?"

Kozol stepped forward. Nina stood between the officer and Tony, her arms folded across her chest.

Detective Fender placed one hand on her shoulder and gently stepped around. "Tony Kozol," he said with obvious relish, "you are under arrest for the murder of Michael Razner. You have the right to remain silent. Anything you say—"

Kozol barely heard the rest. He was instructed to place his hands behind his back. Officer Keyes cuffed Tony and Murchison led him out to a waiting unmarked car. Several of Nina's neighbors gaped in wonder.

Of all the humilities, Nina volunteered to call a lawyer.

"What's this all about?" demanded Tony, indignantly as the unmarked car headed down Sixth Street. Murchison drove. Detective Fender sat along side Murchison up front. Officer Keyes sat next to Kozol.

Detective Fender turned around. "We've found a possible murder weapon in your apartment, counselor. It's enough to charge you. Don't worry, I'm sure you'll find our facilities to your liking."

¤

Tony was placed in a holding cell in the Ocean Palm Police Station. At least they had removed the handcuffs. Kozol waited for over an hour before he was roused by a uniformed guard who led him without word to an interrogation room.

Detective Fender was already seated at the table. He

looked like he wanted to chew off a corner and spit out the pieces. Officer Keyes looked like he'd rather be any place else. Tony took the only other chair in the room and faced the detective.

"You want a lawyer?" spat Fender out of the side of his mouth.

"Are you actually charging me with murder?"

There was a raging silence. Kozol held his breath.

"No," said Fender.

Tony jumped up. "What?"

Fender leaped and pushed Kozol back down to his chair. "Sit," he said with a voice that Tony feared could be lethal.

There were only the three men in the room. Two officers and himself. Kozol knew when not to push. Like Uncle Jonathan used to say, never push if you don't have the room to stand on. Leverage was key to everything.

Tony bided his time.

"We found a .22 in your apartment, wrapped in a gun box, taped shut, on your top closet shelf."

"What the hell were you doing in my apartment?"

"Relax, Kozol. We had a search warrant. All legal-like."

"On what grounds? You have no right to go fishing!"

"We received an anonymous tip that the murder weapon would be found in your apartment. My men and I had no trouble at all finding the weapon." He paused.

Tony squirmed.

"Do you remember when I last asked you if you owned a weapon, Mister Kozol?" said Fender with an unnatural calm.

Tony liked him better when he screamed and cajoled.

It was more in character and easier to understand.

"You said no."

"I forgot," said Kozol. "It belonged to my father. He left it to me when he died. It's one of the few things he had to leave. I couldn't just throw it away. I never think about the thing at all. And I've never fired it—"

"Excuse me, sir." Officer Murchison popped his head through the door.

"What is it, Rocky?"

"About the gun, sir. It's confirmed. The weapon has not been fired recently and it's the wrong caliber. They can run some ballistics tests anyway, if you want—"

Murchison shook his head. "No, don't waste the taxpayers' money, Rocky."

Tony laughed. "I told you!" He rose and dusted off his pants.

"That's all, Rocky," said Detective Fender, by way of dismissal.

Rocky cleared his throat. "Uh, sir, there was one other thing—"

"Well, what is it? I'm not a mind reader."

"The boys figured while they were at the suspect's apartment that they might as well look around some more. He may have more than the one gun after all."

"And?"

"There wasn't," said Rocky, scratching his head. "Another gun, that is."

"What the hell are you trying to say?" said Officer Keyes who had so far remained reasonably quiet.

"Well, behind the dishwasher in the kitchen—Angelo had seen it done on t.v. before, on one of those detective shows, so he figured he'd try it, that is, he pulled out the dishwasher, it comes right out, you know—"

"So?" said Fender.

"So he found a knife."

"A knife?"

"Yes, sir. Wrapped in plastic covered with what look to be blood stains, so he says. Angelo said it was taped to the back of the dishwasher. Damn clever."

Kozol didn't know if Murchison meant this Angelo character or whomever had put the knife behind his dishwasher in the first place.

"They're bringing it in now."

Fender turned and gave Tony a look that the devil himself couldn't have fathomed.

Kozol wasn't feeling so good himself.

Fender tipped back his chair and put his hands over his face, mashing it as if it were made of clay. "So," he said, in a strained, muffled voice, "I've got a victim who's been shot. A suspect with a gun that hasn't been fired and he's hiding a knife covered with blood—" He slammed his open hands against the table and said, "Cut yourself slicing onions, Kozol?"

The table shook.

Tony swallowed. Hard.

"Put him away for the night and tell the county lab that I want the blood results on that knife back as soon as possible."

"Yes, sir," replied Murchison. "That Nina Lasher is here to see him."

"Fine," said Fender, whose face was regaining its original, if not improved, shape. "Give them five minutes.

Then escort Mr. Kozol to his suite."

"Would you care to make a statement?" said Officer Keyes softly.

"No," answered Tony.

"Five minutes," repeated Fender.

Murchison escorted Nina into the interrogation room and locked her and Tony inside alone.

Kozol asked, "What are you doing here?"

"I wanted to see if you were all right."

"Yeah, I'm okay." Tony was silent for a moment. Traps were springing up all around him. One moment he was free, the next arrested for murder.

...And when he thought he was free once more life took another bite out of his behind. If only the police would believe that he was just as baffled as they were. A little help couldn't hurt and, if the girl believed him, maybe somebody else would too.

"Listen," said Kozol, running a hand through his rumpled hair, "do you think you can get me out of here?"

"I asked at the desk. The sergeant said your bail had been set at thirty-five thousand dollars."

"Thirty-five thousand!" Tony gasped. "I'll never be able to pay that!"

Nina pulled a sheet of paper from her purse and said, "Don't worry. If you sign this I'll take care of it."

"What's this?" Kozol asked suspiciously, his eyes skimming the document. "You want me to sign a power of attorney over to you?"

"Yes. If you do, the bondsman will cover your bail. I've already arranged for everything," she said, almost apologetically, "if you agree."

"But the money. You're not thinking of the fifty grand the police say is in my account are you? It's not even mine—"

"No," Nina said. "The restaurant. You're the owner now. You have an equity in the building and business. It's your collateral for bail."

"So," said Tony, sullenly, "if I forfeit bail, I'll lose the restaurant next. Not that I want it, but it's all I've got."

Kozol paced the tiny room. In spite of the air conditioning, he was sweating. Tony's blue suit reeked of fear and fatigue. His whole life was beginning to stink big time. He looked at Nina and considered his choices...all one of them.

Nina said nothing.

Tony reached out his hand. "Fine," he said. "Give me a pen, I'll sign."

Murchison came through the door. "Let's go, Kozol. I'd like to get some sleep myself. Besides, I've got a wife and kids waiting for me."

"How nice for you," Tony said, signing his name quickly to the legal document. "Do give your wife my apologies for any inconveniences I might have caused."

"Shut up, wise ass."

Nina folded the power-of-attorney and replaced it in her purse. "Don't worry," she said in a ridiculously upbeat manner, "you'll be out by morning!"

Kozol nodded as Murchison led him down the long corridor to his cell.

NINE

True to her word, Nina had successfully gotten Tony released the next morning.

Kozol walked out stiffly, his back and legs aching from the unforgiving platform bed he'd spent the night not sleeping on.

Tony's mood was as foul as his suit. He hadn't had a change of clothing in over twenty-four hours. His eyes were puffy and his face pale. His tongue was pasty and he desperately needed a toothbrush.

There was no sparkle in his eyes as he greeted Nina Lasher, but Kozol was grateful to see her nonetheless.

"Thanks," he said in a tired and beaten voice.

"Sure," said Nina in a surprisingly business-like manner.

She was dressed in faded blue jeans, a white t-shirt and canvas high-tops. Her hair hung down loosely. Tony had never seen it like that. Her face looked far less severe, less bookkeeperish.

"Bail's arranged?"

Nina grappled with her purse and said, "Yes and no. You see, I arranged for everything like I said I would. But I was told by the desk sergeant that it is all unnecessary. You've been released and all charges have been dropped. It looks like I went through a lot of work for nothing. I have the papers right here if you want to see them."

"That's okay," said Kozol. "Sorry you had to go through all that hassle over nothing. Let's just get out of here." He opened the door for Nina Lasher.

The desk sergeant said nothing as they walked outside. Tony squinted as his eyes teared up from the intensity of the morning sun. "Where's your car?"

"I've got Leilah's truck," answered Nina. "You left the keys on the counter at my house and I told Leilah we'd bring it back today." She offered Kozol the Snoopy key ring. "Do you want to drive?"

"No, I'm exhausted. I don't think I got more than an hour of uninterrupted sleep last night."

"Worrying too much?"

"Yeah, that and the drunks they kept bringing into the holding cells all night. It's amazing, the number of lushes in this town. Uncle Jonathan should have left me a bar."

Nina unlocked the Jeep's doors and Tony slid gratefully into the passenger's seat. He pushed aside a pile of debris—books, papers, cellophane, a hairbrush, a comb and god-knows-what from the floor to make room for his feet to hit the carpet. He sighed.

"Don't worry," said Nina. "I'm sure you'll work everything out."

"So, you talked to Leilah?" Kozol inquired, as Nina headed out into traffic.

"Yes."

"Does she know I've been arrested?"

"I hope you don't mind," replied Nina. "Everybody's concerned about you. Besides, I needed her help digging up the papers on the restaurant so I could arrange bail."

"It's a little embarrassing, that's all," said Tony, squirming in his seat.

"I don't see why," said Nina, diffidently. "I mean, we all know you're a murder suspect already. Now you've simply been charged with the crime."

"Gee, I guess that makes it all right then." Kozol managed a weak laugh, despite his troubles.

Nina patted Tony's leg. "That's the spirit. I'm sure you'll beat the rap, as they say."

"Yeah, I hope so." Kozol kicked at the garbage on the floor with the toe of his shoe. A flash of lilac caught his eye. He bent and picked up a book of matches. "That's funny."

"What is?" asked Nina, taking her eyes from the road ahead to see what Tony was doing.

"This matchbook."

"Leilah smokes. You know that. It's a nasty habit though."

"Yeah, but this is a matchbook from Girls Galore."

"Girls Galore?"

"That's one of Razner's clubs. It's where Pamela works."

"Oh." Nina glanced his way again. "How can you tell it's from there? I don't see any writing on it."

"The matchbooks don't have the Girls Galore name on them but I'd swear it's from there. I've seen enough of them." Kozol examined the matchbook inside and out. "The color of the matchbooks is the same shade purple as the club. Razner thought it was more classy that way. Besides, if some nosey housewife found a pack of matches in some poor slob's pants, she wouldn't get suspicious or bent out of shape like she would if it had the name of the strip club emblazoned on its cover."

"Could be Leilah knows something."

"Maybe," agreed Nina, "or maybe it's only some other purple colored matchbook."

Tony was forced to agree. Yet still he found it curious. "Yeah. Listen," he said, "you mind swinging by my place first? We pass it on the way to the restaurant and I'd like to change into some clean clothes."

"No, I don't mind. Which way?"

Kozol gave her directions. He was about to tell Nina to park in his parking space but his own car was already parked there. On four good tires.

"Hey, I got my car back!" He told Nina to instead park in front of the building in one of the open spaces reserved for guests. Tony put the matchbook in his coat pocket.

"Come on, I'm on the third floor." He led her through the entryway to the elevators. His front door was out in the corridor, leaning forlornly against the wall. There was a big X of yellow and black police tape crossing his doorway that wouldn't have intimidated a toddler.

"Great," muttered Kozol.

"What happened? Did the police do this when they searched your apartment?"

"Yes and no." Tony explained how Officer Keyes had earlier smashed in his door. "So," he explained, "they didn't have to so much as knock when they came to search the place. I told the superintendent to fix it yesterday. Looks like he never got around to it."

Kozol caught Mrs. Pikipsky staring at them. "Can I help you?" he asked sternly.

Mrs. Pikipsky stood all of four and a half feet tall. She had to be over seventy years old. Tony barely spoke to her. She seemed never to leave her apartment except to spy through the crack of her door. Mrs. Pikipsky was wearing a house robe. It was blue, which complimented her hair. Her teeth were yellow and big. Like Chiclets.

"Bringing another one home?" Mrs. Pikipsky said in a disdainful tone as her eyes went up and down Nina. "Watch out, sugar," she warned. "He's a murderer you know!" Her crooked finger pointed accusingly at Tony.

Kozol stepped forward and said, "Boo!"

Mrs. Pikipsky turned and retreated behind her front door. Tony heard the sound of a lock turning and a chain being pushed securely into place.

Nina laughed.

"Come on," said Kozol, breaking away the tape with his hand. He took a look around the apartment. It was worse than he'd imagined. The now famous dishwasher was in the middle of the kitchen floor, standing in a puddle of water. Nothing was where it used to be.

And the television, a forty-two inch with high definition, was nowhere. And he still owed fifty-six dollars a month for the next thirty-four months on it.

Worst of all, his prized possession, a Martin D-28

acoustic guitar, which his father had bequeathed him, lay in the middle of the living room. Its neck had been broken. Tony suppressed the urge to cry.

"You know," said Nina, stepping over an overturned chair, "if your door was broken already, anybody could have gotten in here and placed that knife the police are talking about. You weren't even home all day."

"That's right," said Tony, rising out of the fog of his shock. He felt like an idiot for not having thought of that earlier. "Hell, anybody could have planted the knife. They didn't even have to break in. Walk right in, take your time, find a good spot, hide the knife and leave. Then call the police—"

"—Anonymously."

"Yeah, anonymously. And I'm left hanging."

"It certainly sounds like someone is out to frame you, Tony." Nina picked up the chair and arranged it neatly beside a walnut end table. "Go ahead and get changed if you like. I'll straighten up here a bit."

"You don't have to do that," said Kozol.

"That's okay. I don't mind." Her gaze fell on the bloody footprints.

Tony quickly explained. "I cut myself in the shower, a cup broke you see and—"

"Sure," Nina said, "of course. I suppose that could happen..."

"I mean, it's not like I murdered somebody here if that's what you're thinking." He lifted his foot. "I'll show you where I cut myself."

"Never mind," Nina said hastily. "Anyway, you'd better phone your building manager and insist that he fix your front door."

"Right. Though it didn't do any good when I called earlier. It always takes ages to get anything done around here."

Nina scooped up a pile of sports magazines and dumped then on the coffee table. "Be forceful," she told Tony. "Threaten him. Tell him you'll sue. Tell him you hold him responsible for any personal damages or lost property."

Tony picked up his broken guitar and laid it lovingly down atop a couple of overturned sofa cushions, then went to the phone.

Kozol dialed the building manager's number. It was on a list of telephone numbers stuck to the refrigerator. As he dialed, Tony came to the discomforting realization that had Nina chosen to be a lawyer, she would have been a better one than he himself had so far been.

Maybe he should have stuck with his music. He wasn't half bad as a guitar player. After all, he had managed to make something of a living playing guitar in bar bands when he was in college and, later still, in law school. Some of his friends played professionally.

Being a lawyer had seemed like a more grown up profession at the time. Now, he wasn't so sure. Besides, most of his peers were busy manipulating the justice system to fill their own already overstuffed pockets. None seemed interested in justice as a cause.

Maybe it had become unfashionable.

¤

Nina and Kozol didn't leave until the carpenter had secured the door to its frame. Mr. Wagner, the superintendent, promised to send the painter first thing in the morning to finish the job. He'd even changed the lock. Tony put the new key on his ring.

"At least you won't have to worry about anyone strolling in," Nina said as Kozol locked the door behind them.

He jiggled the handle just to be sure. "Yeah. They'll have to break in if they want to try to plant any more evidence and even the Ocean Palm police won't be able to ignore that. Though I can't imagine why anybody would plant some strange bloody knife in my apartment. The police are sure that Razner was shot."

"Maybe whoever is trying to frame you isn't the same person as committed the murder and the police don't know that," suggested Nina as they rode down in the elevator.

The elevator car went down but Tony's head started going in circles. "God, don't even start thinking that way," he groaned. "I'm getting a headache at the mere suggestion."

Kozol stared at the lighted green numbers on the wall panel as they flashed logically and smoothly down to one. "Somehow I've got to get this all sorted out though."

Hand in pocket, Tony jiggled the unmarked lilac matchbook which he'd transferred to his clean trousers. "Somehow."

TEN

Tony happily drove his own car to the Dairy Delites. He'd found a bill from the towing company stuck to the inside of the dash. Sixty-five dollars for a house call and it wasn't even his house. The tow operator had added a notation that the Saab needed the passenger's side window mechanism checked out.

Like Tony didn't know it.

Oh well, the car rode like a dream otherwise, though the brakes were a little spongy. Nina Lasher followed in Leilah's Jeep Cherokee. The parking lot at the Dairy Delites was pretty crowded. That was a good sign. But then it was lunch time.

Nina and Kozol strapped on aprons over their clothes and pitched in, dishing out burgers and drinks, matching customers to their orders.

"Listen, I'd like to talk to you, Leilah," said Tony, leaning over the girl's shoulder where she stood at the register handing out change to a customer.

"About what?" asked Leilah, as she gave a five dollar bill and some coins over to a young woman in a postal workers' uniform.

"About these," revealed Kozol. He'd pulled the lilac colored matchbook from his pocket and held it out for Leilah to see.

Her eyes sharpened reflexively, but barely. Still Tony hadn't missed it. As an attorney he'd seen that look before, from clients confronted with a dredged up truth they'd rather have ignored.

"I don't know what your talking about," she replied in an even tone. Leilah shoved the drawer of the cash register in with more force than necessary.

"I've got patties piling up!" screamed Joe impatiently.

"Later."

"These look like the same matches—"

"Later, I said," Leilah replied snappishly. "May I help you?" she asked, focusing her eyes on the next customer in line.

"Yes, tell me," began the teenager, "does the deluxe combo come with soda?"

Kozol scowled and returned to the business at hand. Leilah was evading him but she couldn't go on that way forever. He wanted answers.

"Oh-oh," said Leilah, sometime later as the crowd faded.

"What's wrong?" Tony asked, wiping his forehead with a damp handkerchief.

"It's Mrs. Carlotti."

"So?" Kozol watched the spry looking older woman as

she climbed slowly out a largish four door sedan. She was wearing an orange blossom print dress with sturdy brown, low heeled shoes. Her skin was loose and also brown. Her hair was thin and gray, held back with a white headband. "She looks harmless enough. What's her story?"

"She's an old windbag," put in Joe. He rolled the spatula along the grease track and turned down the flames. He'd put a stack of half-cooked burgers in the warmer and wouldn't need to cook much for a while in the expected lull between lunch and dinner. "The old bag is nothing but grief. Grief and trouble. Don't worry, boss, I'll send the bitch packing!" Joe squared his shoulders as if preparing to toss the old woman out on her ear.

Tony was horrified. "Listen, Joe, thanks, but I'll handle this. Why don't you go ahead and take a break. You've earned it."

Joe grinned and nodded. "Yeah, I have."

Joe was quick to agree when it suited him. He scooped up a wrapped burger and filled his soda cup with ice tea.

"Where's Jonathan?" The voice cracked like a piece of old glass that's been lying in the outdoors and carelessly stepped on with a rubber shoe.

"He's not here any longer," Kozol said with a smile. "Can I be of assistance?" He held out his hand.

Mrs. Carlotti ignored it. And him.

The infamous Mrs. Carlotti looked at Leilah and said, "He can't hide, girlie. He can't hide."

"I'm in charge now, Mrs. Carlotti," Tony cut in. "What seems to be the problem?"

"I'm dying! That's the problem, pretty boy," she said whippishly.

"Mrs. Carlotti used to be a regular customer of Jonathan's," explained Leilah. "Until she says she was diagnosed with cancer—"

"Says?" interjected the old woman, indignantly. "I do have cancer! Everywhere! And it's your food that's done it!"

Kozol thought the old woman seemed spry enough and healthy enough. Healthy enough to stir up trouble at the very least.

"Mrs. Carlotti thinks our food caused her cancer," further explained Leilah, all the while giving the woman a stony eyed glare.

"Poisoned me, that's what you did! Now where's Jonathan?"

Tony asked, "What is it exactly that you wish to see Jonathan for?"

"If he doesn't come up with some money to pay my medical bills, I'm going to sue him, that's what for, pretty boy."

She'd said the pretty boy part with an extra ounce of venom. That's what was bugging Kozol the most.

"Mrs. Carlotti," Tony began in a firm but even tone, "surely you don't believe that because you may have eaten some meals here that our food is responsible for your cancer? I guarantee you, all our beef and our produce is government inspected—"

Kozol shot off vague assurances, the veracity of which he had no idea.

"If she even has cancer," Leilah chided. "I think it's the mad cow disease."

Mrs. Carlotti hissed, more like a cobra snake than a

cow, mad or otherwise. "You little hussy!"

"Now, now," said Tony, trying to placate and then quickly get rid of the old woman without upsetting the rest of his customers. "I'm afraid Jonathan, my uncle, really isn't here. You may not have heard, but he and Aunt Louise have gone off on a cruise."

Kozol did not mention the inheritance Uncle Jonathan had received. He figured Mrs. Carlotti would soon try to get her claws on it if he had. She seemed the type.

Tony tried another tack. "You see, my uncle's been gone almost a week, Mrs. Carlotti. Perhaps you would like to discuss this matter with him yourself when he returns?"

"Nonsense," countered Mrs. Carlotti. Her tongue was pasty white and wildly shot out of her withered mouth whenever she said a word that began with the letter N. "I saw him in that shiny white Cadillac of his only yesterday. Man can afford to pay my medical bills. Been poisoning my body for years."

"You must be mistaken. There are lots of Cadillacs on the road, especially white ones down here in Florida."

"I know what I saw, pretty boy."

Kozol didn't know what to say.

"Get out of here, granny!" yelled Joe, turning the corner. "Why don't you go hustle up a game of bingo down at the church with your friends? It ought to be easy to cheat those old buggers out of some quarters. They can't hear. They can't see. That's more your speed. Go on! Bother somebody else for a change!"

"Why you horrid little—" Mrs. Carlotti huffed and abruptly turned her back.

"Just don't die," hollered Joe, through a mouthful of

burger, "because we love you just the way you are, grandma!"

Poor Mrs. Carlotti scuttled out the door. Joe faced Tony and said smugly, "It's the only way to handle them."

For once, Kozol had to agree with him.

"That's it. I'm out of here," said Leilah. She reached behind, untied her apron and tossed it under the counter.

"Not so fast, Leilah," Tony said. "I want to talk to you."

Leilah looked at him defiantly. "I have to go to the bathroom. Care to follow me?"

"Yes, I do."

Leilah marched past the counter, around the back, out to the dining room toward the ladies room in the far corner of the restaurant. Kozol followed closely.

"You coming?" Leilah said with a smile, holding the women's room door wide open. A startled middle-aged woman busily reapplying her mascara threw her makeup kit into her purse and pushed past them.

Said Tony firmly, "I'll be waiting right here." He knew his limits and women's bathrooms were one of them.

"Gee, are you sure you can trust me? Maybe I'll climb out the window and make a break for it like they do in the movies."

Kozol shook his head. "There are no windows," he said confidently.

"You are a pain in the ass, pretty boy—" Leilah let the door swing closed behind her.

Tony squelched his rage. He slid into the nearest booth and waited. Much to Kozol's chagrin it was Detective Fender who suddenly appeared at the dining room door and made his way toward him.

Tony closed his fist around the Girls Galore match-book. It wasn't something Fender needed to know about.

"I hope you're here to buy something," Kozol said, looking forlornly at the nearly empty dining area.

"Nah, are you kidding? I heard they found a dead body in the freezer. Now I ask you, how sanitary is that?"

"If you don't keep your voice down I'll sue you for slander." Tony was getting quite sick of Detective Fender and his mouth.

"Good luck," said Fender with a smirk. "I hear it's hard as hell to find an ethical lawyer in this town though." Fender stuffed himself into the booth opposite Kozol.

Fender pulled two Dairy Delites napkins out of the chrome dispenser and blew his nose.

"Those are for the paying customers."

"Leilah Merchant working here today?" Detective Fender tossed the soiled, wet napkins down on the table and shoved them out of his way with the back of his hand.

"Leilah? Matter of fact," said Tony, not even trying to hide his disgust for the man, "she is. What do you want to talk to her for?" Kozol was surprised to find himself taking a protective, paternalistic attitude toward his employees. It was an attitude Tony didn't think he, as a businessman, could afford.

Fender smiled enigmatically. "Police business," he answered. "Where is she?" He looked over his shoulder.

"Bathroom."

Fender nodded. "Funny business about that knife of yours—" he said as they waited.

"Anybody could have planted it. Your men broke

down my door, remember? I only got it fixed today."

"Tsk, tsk. Only trying to save your life is all they were doing. Is this the thanks they get?"

Kozol ignored Fender's baiting comments. "For all I know that knife could've belonged to the tenant before me."

"Blood was too fresh for that. Any other ideas, Sherlock?"

Before Tony could answer, Leilah appeared at the restroom door.

"What's this? Call for police backup?"

"Afternoon, Miss Merchant," said Detective Fender. He shifted to the back of the booth. "I have a few questions I need to ask of you. Take a seat."

Leilah looked from one man to the other as if considering her chances and then pushed in next to Tony. "Like what?" she asked bluntly.

"Did you know the victim, Michael Razner?" he asked point-blank.

"No."

Fender pulled a folded sheet of paper from the outside pocket of his sports coat. He spread it open on the tabletop and turned it so Leilah and Kozol could both read it.

"What's all this?" Tony demanded to know. Leilah stayed conspicuously silent.

"Ran a background check on everybody here. Just routine."

"So?"

"This is a copy of a police report from Miami Beach," said the detective. "Seems Leilah took a shot at a man down on South Beach a little more than a month ago. Didn't hit him, luckily, but the police were called and a report was filed. The gentleman refused to file a complaint. Miss Merchant was charged with unlawful discharge of a firearm. Care to guess who that man was, Kozol?"

Tony was dumbfounded. "Michael Razner?"

"The one and only."

Leilah said, her voice almost a whisper, "I wasn't trying to kill him. I was angry, I only wanted to scare the bastard."

"You mean you knew him?" Kozol asked. He looked at her incredulously. It seemed wholly out of character with the Leilah Tony thought he was beginning to know.

"Yeah," nodded Leilah. "I'd been seeing him on and off."

"For how long?" asked Detective Fender.

Leilah shrugged. "About six months, I suppose."

Lord, thought Kozol, was there a woman Razner had not slept with?

"And where did the two of you meet originally?"

"Here," said Leilah, "at the Dairy Delites."

"What! When we found the body you said you'd never seen him before. What were you—"

"Quiet, Kozol!" snapped the detective. "This is my investigation. Go ahead," he said to Leilah.

Leilah folded her hands. "That's all there is. Michael used to come in every so often. We got to talking. He made me laugh. After a while, he asked me out. And," she said, "he gave me money." Her eyes avoided both men.

Tony wasn't sure, but there might have been tears

forming at the corners of her eyes.

"I don't make a lot. Obviously. It helped out." Leilah was surprisingly acquiescent.

"But he was married! Didn't you know that?"

"Kozol—" warned Fender in a voice that came out as a deep, drawn out drawl.

"I knew. He told me. Didn't seem too worried about it though. I don't think his wife knew. Michael didn't talk about her much."

"How often did Mister Razner come here?" Fender asked.

"Maybe once every month or two."

"What the hell would a guy like Razner be coming here for?" Tony asked. "I mean, who are we kidding, the food's not that great."

"He and Jonathan knew one another," explained Leilah. "Mostly they went upstairs and talked for a while and then Michael would leave."

"Jonathan? My Uncle Jonathan? I don't believe it," said Tony, shaking his head in utter astonishment.

Fender gave Kozol a look that shut him up. "What was your fight about on South Beach?"

Leilah explained. "I told Michael I didn't want to see him anymore. I was tired of it. I felt so dirty. Michael laughed and told me that 'his' women weren't allowed to leave him." Leilah bit her lower lip. "It was then I realized what a real jerk he was. I kept a gun in my purse. Michael was laughing at me like some stupid wise ass son-of-a-bitch."

Leilah's voice rose nervously as she spoke. "So I pulled out my revolver and blew off a round past his ear."

Fender laughed. "Man, you're one crazy lady," he said. "According to the statements you and Mister Razner gave the police that night on South Beach, Razner grabbed the gun from you and threw it in the ocean. Yet none of the witnesses questioned could verify that."

He looked steadily at Leilah. "The gun was never recovered."

Tony asked, "Do you think that's the gun that killed Razner?"

"Where is your gun, Miss Merchant?"

"Glove box," she said with a voice like a deflated balloon. "But I didn't kill anybody. Michael never threw my gun away. He just took out the bullets and gave it back to me."

"What caliber is the weapon?" Fender asked.

"Thirty-eight."

"Same as killed Razner. Ballistics should prove interesting." Fender folded up the police report and replaced it in his pocket. "Can you account for your whereabouts when Michael Razner was murdered?"

"From what I've heard, you don't even know when he was murdered," replied Leilah, with a hint of her usual toughness coming through.

Fender stared her down.

Leilah caved. "It doesn't matter, anyway," she replied. "I was home every night."

"Any way to prove that?" Fender's voice was stony, testy.

"Yes. I live with my dad."

"Does he work? Would he know when you're in or out?"

"Daddy's always in the apartment. He's got MS."

"MS?"

"Multiple sclerosis. He's going through a bad time of it now, too. And his medical bills are ridiculous, even with his pension and my pay. That's why I kept seeing Michael. We needed that money."

"And you believe your father will vouch for your whereabouts?"

"That's right."

"Of course, he is your father."

Leilah smirked. "He's also a twenty year veteran," she said. "He had to take early retirement on account of his being struck with the MS. Broke his heart to retire. Daddy was only forty when it first came on."

"Army?" asked Fender.

"Nope," Leilah replied, the smirk never left her face, "City of Detroit Police Department. Lieutenant Merchant."

Fender looked like an angler whose once-in-a-lifetime catch had just slipped away, off the hook, below the surface, slipped away, far away. He scratched his head. "I'll need that gun," Fender said. "And I'll have a word with your father."

Leilah rose. "Like I said, the gun is in the car."

Detective Fender rose and followed her out. At the door he paused and said to Tony, "Sorry, looks like you're my only partner for this dance, Kozol," and departed.

Tony opened his hand. He stared at the crumpled matchbook in his palm, waiting for it to go up in flames, like his life.

ELEVEN

Kozol dialed the Goodwill offices from the phone in the back storeroom. He'd gotten the telephone number off the Goodwill drop off box in the parking lot on his way in. "Hello, Goodwill? I need somebody to—"

"One moment please."

Tony waited. Considerably more than a moment. He'd parked next to the Goodwill clothing drop off box on his way in and realized then that the box itself was the source of the ever increasing odor that everybody from customers to employees had been complaining about.

The drop off box had been there, beside a parking lamp, in the shopping center's lot for as many years as Kozol could remember. Tony was beginning to wonder just how long it had been since someone had last picked up clothing from that particular location.

"May I help you?" asked a woman's voice.

"Yes, my name is Tony Kozol. I'm the owner of a

restaurant, Dairy Delites Ice Cream Parlor and Barbecue in Ocean Palm. There's a Goodwill box out here in the parking lot and I was wondering—"

"What is the box number please?"

"Number?"

"Yes," replied the disembodied voice, like a school teacher instructing her most difficult pupil, "there should be an identification number along the—"

"I don't know. It's here in the Ocean Palm Shopping Center. You can't miss it. Take a deep breath, you can probably smell it from there!"

"Really! There's no need to be rude, sir. This is a charitable organization, you know," the woman answered sharply. "Our drop boxes provide a useful service to the community."

Tony apologized. "I know. Listen, I'm sorry. I think it might be full, that's all. And it really does smell. It's driving away the customers. All those clothes— probably mildewing and molding out there in the heat. The clothes could be going bad. Can't you send someone to pick it up?" pleaded Kozol.

"I'll make a mention of it to our driver. What is your name and address again, please?"

Tony told her both and hoped for the best. Armed with a fresh can of Lysol and prepared to empty all of its contents into the bin through the metal hatch, he approached the wicked smelling Goodwill box.

Leilah and Detective Fender were still conversing by the side of Leilah's Jeep.

"You mind letting her get back to work?" Kozol shouted across the parking lot. He saw Fender say something to the girl, then head his way. Leilah locked the Cherokee and headed back towards Dairy Delites.

"She smells pretty ripe," said Fender, sucking noisily on a toothpick.

"No kidding." The drop off box was a sturdy metal rectangle over six feet high and about four feet across. And she did smell pretty ripe. Tony lifted the hatch, held his breath and started spraying. He squirted several times, coughed and retreated. Coughing some more.

"I've asked the Goodwill to get rid of it, or at the least come and pick up the contents."

Fender nodded. "I don't think she did it."

"What?"

"The girl, Leilah Merchant."

"Oh. No, I don't think she did it either." Kozol pulled in several deep, controlled breaths and prepared for another assault on the metal box. His fingers carried the scent of Lysol.

"Whew," complained Fender. He waved a hand in front of his face. "That thing is a public hazard. I ought to cite you for it."

"It isn't mine," said Tony. "This isn't even my property. All this parking belongs to the shopping center. So go ahead and cite the management. Maybe then we can get rid of this damned box for good!" Kozol squinched up his face as he blasted the can a second time with Lysol.

Tony asked between breaths, "Don't you have some police work to do?" He sprayed the last of the Lysol and tossed the empty can inside.

Detective Fender laughed. "I like watching you squirm. Besides," he said, as he extracted the wet toothpick from his mouth, scratched the side of his head and returned the toothpick to his lips, "there's something about that smell." The detective stepped closer, inched open the chute and took a little sniff. "You know," he said, "I had a case once about six years ago. Man killed his wife and stuffed her body in the trunk of his car. Abandoned the car out at the mall. Guess he figured no one would notice for a long time. It was the stench that gave it away. Body ripens real fast down here in Florida."

Kozol wondered where Detective Fender was going with his story. "Yeah, well, that's fascinating and I'd love to hear about all your cases, Fender, but I've got a business to run."

"Hold on a second," said Fender. "There a door to this thing?"

Tony said, "Who cares? Let's get out of here and leave the Goodwill to handle this."

"In a minute, counselor." Detective Fender circled the drop off box. "Here it is."

Kozol followed. There was a door built into the backside, probably for the Goodwill driver to handily empty its contents. The rusted chrome handle had a lock in its middle. Like a belly button.

"It's probably locked anyway," said Tony. "Let's get out of here."

Fender's toothpick moved up and down. "Looks broken to me," he said. Using his index finger, the detective tried the handle. It turned easily and the door fell open.

Air, warm and damp, swept over them. It was foul. Big, dark blue flies buzzed the men angrily. Kozol fought them off. "I'm going to be sick," he complained.

The clothes were piled deep. Fender lifted back the topmost and exposed a bloated head and shoulders.

Tony whispered, "Roamie."

"Throat's been cut," said Fender, matter-of-factly.

There was an open paper sack from Dairy Delites beside the body with the remains of a burger and fries slowly being eaten away by a trail of ants. The flies seemed to prefer the body.

Fender turned toward Kozol. "You'll fry for this one, Kozol. Might even get you for a double homicide. Now maybe if you plead guilty on the first one—"

"What are you talking about?" demanded Tony in awe. "You don't think I killed him?" Kozol took a step backward. "I was with you when you found the body!"

"First," said Fender, sticking out a finger, "you tried to cover up the smell. Second," he said, holding up another finger, "you told me yourself that you wanted them to get rid of this box for good."

Tony's body chilled with every point Fender raised.

"Third," Detective Fender said, "if the blood on the knife we found in your apartment matches the victim-Bingo!"

Kozol clutched his stomach and vomited the remains of his lunch. It didn't help matters that the contents fell mostly on Fender's shoes.

¤

Nina had him out of jail in two days.

"How'd you manage it?" Tony asked. She led him by

the hand out to her car, a blue Saturn. Practical and not too flashy, like her.

"Remember those papers you signed before? The power of attorney?"

"Right."

Nina unlocked her car door and they climbed inside. The cool air blowing from the car's vents was a relief. The Ocean Palm jail cells were notably warm. Though the rooms where the policemen toiled had seemed cool enough to Kozol on his last visit.

"Well, I still had them in my purse. But your bail was set at seventy-five thousand this time. And I couldn't raise that much on the restaurant alone."

"The bank money?"

"I'm afraid so. I had to use it otherwise you'd be held over at County until the trial."

Tony had no doubt about what a little hell that would have been. "You did the right thing, but I don't know how you managed."

"I managed."

"Thanks for getting me out. With Uncle Jonathan and Aunt Louise out of town I didn't have anyone else to turn to."

"No problem." Nina slowed to let a young jogger cross the road. "Fender and Keyes tried to talk me out of it though. They think you're a crazed lunatic and that the world would be safer with you behind bars."

"I'm not surprised."

"You really should get a good lawyer, Tony. The way Fender and Keyes explained it, they really have a strong case against you."

"Don't tell me they've got you believing their stories?"

"No," Nina said bluntly. "I told them you'd have to be pretty stupid to have committed both those murders in that fashion and that I didn't think you were that dumb."

"Thanks, I think," answered Kozol.

"You're welcome."

"How's everything at Dairy Delites?" Tony suddenly felt that a change of subjects was in order. Kozol had worried the whole time he was locked up. He needed the money from the restaurant now as much as ever.

"Good. Everyone's been pitching in. Leilah's been handling the personnel. I've been taking care of the money side of things."

Kozol nodded. The business was probably in better hands than his. "Has there been any word from Uncle Jonathan?"

"Nothing but a postcard that came yesterday from your Aunt Louise saying the ship would be in Panama for six days."

"Six days," said Tony. "Maybe I can reach them at their hotel. Did she say which one?"

"No, she only said she hoped you two were getting along. The postcard itself is a snapshot of the Panama Canal back when it was under construction. Not much help there."

"Two?"

"I thought maybe she was talking about your girl-friend."

"No, that can't be. At least, I don't think so. My fiancé broke up with me when I lost my license."

"Sorry."

There was an awkward silence as Kozol tried to assess his next move.

"You should show Detective Fender the postcard. Maybe the police can find your aunt and uncle through the Embassy or something."

Tony said, "I guess there's not much to lose."

"Leilah's been cleared, you know."

"Yeah, Fender told me. The ballistics didn't match up. Not that I expected they would. But that goddamn knife with Roamie's blood on it— the police have identified it as a knife from Uncle Jonathan's, I mean, my restaurant. Several people at Dairy Delites recognized it as one of our produce knives. The Medical Examiner swears it's the murder weapon, too. There were no prints on it though.

Thank God for that. I mean, the way things are going I expected they'd find my prints on the damn thing. After all, just about everybody in the restaurant has handled those knives. My luck, I'd have the only recognizable set of prints."

"Something will turn up, Tony."

"I sure wish I could get a hold of Uncle Jonathan," Kozol said. "The police had already been trying to locate him and take his statement. It's not easy without the name of the ship. I told Detective Fender to try the travel agencies and he laughed in my face. He asked me if I happened to know just how many millions of travel agencies there were in south Florida alone."

"He's right there. It won't be easy."

"Yeah, but the postcard could help. Uncle Jonathan might be able to clear a lot of this up for me. At least about Michael Razner. I can't for the life of me figure out the connection between those two. Why would Razner visit Uncle Jonathan once every month or two like Leilah said?"

"Friends maybe?" voiced Nina.

"Hard to imagine. They had nothing in common that I can think of and surely Uncle Jonathan wouldn't have been comfortable with what Razner did for a living."

"You're probably right," Nina admitted.

"My luck, the police can't even find cousin Scott."

"Why not? You said he was at the University of Miami."

"According to his roommate he hooked up with a new girl and he's taken the semester off to go hiking about Europe."

The Saturn came to a stop.

"What about this," began Nina, as they sat waiting at the rail crossing while the green and white Tri-Rail went by on one its many daily shuttles, "did you ever wonder why Michael Razner picked you to be his lawyer before? I mean, no offense, but like you said yourself, you were nobody. Razner could afford the priciest, biggest names in Florida. Yet he hired you."

Tony tried his best not be insulted, but it was hard. "And you think Uncle Jonathan might have had something to do with me getting the job?"

"It is a possibility, right? Razner knowing your uncle and you suddenly getting hired by a notorious big shot that you don't even know. Maybe your uncle got Razner to do him a favor."

Kozol agreed. "That might explain it. Not that it has been much of a favor."

Nina shrugged. "Your uncle had no way of knowing how things would turn out." The crossing gate arm rose. Traffic surged forward. "Which way?"

"Drop me off at my apartment, would you? I need to get my car and then go over to work."

"Your Saab? It's still parked outside the Dairy Delites."

"Oh, that's right. Let's go on over, then."

Nina parked beside the neglected Saab. There was a coat of smeared blackish dust covering the vehicle from bumper to bumper. And several birds had managed bulls-eyes. The inside windows were fogged over.

"It rained yesterday," Nina said. "I had Joe run out to close your windows but he said the one wouldn't go up."

"It's broken," explained Tony. "Joe put the plastic up?"

"Yes, that's why it's all fogged up inside, I suppose."

Kozol inspected the translucent, layered plastic that had been affixed with inch wide masking tape along the perimeter of the window. "He did a good job," admitted Tony.

They crossed the parking lot. Kozol held the door open for Nina then stepped inside the Dairy Delites himself. Joe gave him a leer and looked pointedly to his left.

Pamela sat at the first barstool. She wore a pair of faded denim short-shorts and a red tube top with black high-heeled shoes. A slender gold chain hung around her neck, another tinier version, circled her left ankle.

"Hi, Tony," she said with a smile that reached all the way to his nether parts.

"Hi," answered Kozol with surprise. "What are you

doing here?"

Pamela gave him a friendly hug and didn't let go. "I came to see you, baby. I heard they were releasing you. I missed you," she said. Pamela ran a warm slender finger over his suddenly dry lips.

"Well—" said Tony.

"Perhaps you'd like to go over the invoices now, Tony? There's a lot to catch up on since you've been gone," interrupted Nina in her most officious manner.

Pamela cut her off with a move as swift and sure as a body check. "Oh, not now, honey, okay?"

Nina reddened.

"I'd like to visit with Tony awhile. If that's okay with you, baby?" Pamela pressed against Kozol. Her arms circled his waist. Tony felt her hip bones pressing his thighs.

"Well, I suppose," said Kozol, turning to Nina, "it can wait. Can't it, Miss Lasher?"

"Of course," Nina replied stiffly. She turned sharply on her heels and marched off.

"Is there somewhere we can be alone here?" Pamela asked with a voice as smooth and golden as grade A honey.

"There's the office, upstairs."

Pamela allowed Tony to take her hand and lead the way.

TWELVE

"**I** did miss you," cooed Pamela. She sat on the dilapidated sofa, staring doe-eyed up at Kozol who had taken the chair at the desk.

He noticed that everything had been organized. Nina Lasher's doing no doubt. Pamela's legs were crossed and her denim cutoffs rose to her crotch.

"Don't you miss me, baby?"

"You set me up with Razner, Pamela. I've been disbarred. I can't even apply to be reinstated for five years!" Tony stood and paced the small, windowless room.

"People can change, baby. Give me another chance. I have a good heart." Pamela rolled her tube top down to her midriff, exposing her bare tits. "See?"

Kozol saw.

Pamela pulled Tony down on top of her and thrust her tongue deep into his mouth. Her warm lips covered his own with moist, electrical pleasure. Pamela led his hands to her full breasts. Her hand found a hard spot between his legs.

Kozol heard the sudden, staccato stomping of feet up the wooden stairs. The door burst open.

"What's up? You wanted to see me boss?" Joe said eagerly.

Tony leaped from the couch. "Joe!" he hollered. His heart raced in his chest, but it wasn't because of Joe. "What the hell are you doing here?"

"I'm sorry," said Joe, looking totally confused and flustered. That is, even more so than usual. "You said you wanted to see me."

"I never said I wanted to see you!" Kozol leaned against the desk and struggled to catch his breath. "Where'd you get that idea?"

Joe's confusion seemed complete. "Nina said—"

Pamela slowly pulled her top back up over her breasts. She stood and kissed Tony once quickly on the cheek, then again on the lips. This time more slowly. "I'd better go. You call me, baby."

Kozol nodded. Pamela turned and left. Tony watched her alluring backside until it was gone then turned his attention to Joe's rather unflattering mug.

"Hey-hey. Way to go, boss!" Joe gave his boss the thumbs-up sign. "You don't mind me saying so—she's hot!"

Kozol scowled. "And just what was it that I wanted to see you about?"

"I don't know," said Joe. "Don't you know?"

¤

STIFF IN THE FREEZER

Leilah and Nina were up front, huddled around the cash register, chatting about god-knows-what. The place was deader than a morgue. But then, of course, it pretty much had been one of late.

"You're in charge," Tony said sharply.

"Where are you going?" Leilah asked.

"To see Mrs. Razner," Kozol answered.

"What? Are you crazy? What do you want to do that for? Fender's out to fry you. Stay away," warned Leilah.

"I've got to go. Maybe she knows something about Uncle Jonathan's relationship with her dead husband."

"Man, I don't know if you're a murderer or not, but you're crazy enough to be one," Leilah opined.

Nina just looked at him.

Tony glared back at her then headed for the door. He tore the plastic off the broken passenger side window to let the fresh air in and coaxed his nearly dead Saab back to life.

Kozol cut off a slow moving truck that stalled his progress and sped off toward Mrs. Razner's house. It was time to take control and find some answers.

There was a young woman guarding the gate house this time. She was shaped like a bowling pin with a Moe Howard haircut.

"I'm sorry, you're not on the list," she said, firmly, after scrolling her computer screen.

"But if you could call Mrs. Razner and tell her that Tony Kozol is at the gate and needs a word with her. It's urgent—"

The guard shook her head resolutely. "Sorry. Mrs. Razner has left word that she's not to be disturbed and no one is to get through except the realtor. You'll have to turn around."

"Realtor?"

"Yeah, guess she's selling."

A car horn honked impatiently.

"If you don't mind—" The guard made a swirling motion with her hand.

By now several cars had cued up behind the Saab. "There's no room," said Tony.

The girl sighed as if the weight of her job were too heavy. She pushed a button. "Go on through and come out the other side," she said as the gate slowly swung open.

Kozol smiled and waved. And raced straight for Michael Razner's house.

"Hey!" the guard shouted in apparent astonishment. "Stop. Turn around!"

The house was quiet. Like the rest of the neighborhood. There was a Cadillac and Lexus in the open garage. A black Camaro blocked the drive. Tony wondered if it was Pamela's. He had a feeling she was up to something.

Nina might be right. Pamela could have killed Razner. She was ambitious and hungry.

Kozol knew better than to think that she was interested in a disbarred attorney with no money and no prospects. But why all the interest in her dead lover's widow?

There was no sign of Mitch. But that didn't mean anything. The oaf could be creeping behind the bushes or peeping out the curtains. Tony decided to chance it.

Cautiously.

STIFF IN THE FREEZER

He left his car with the key in the ignition and scooted to the side of the house, checking every few seconds for sounds or nosy neighbors.

There were none.

The side of the house was flat, green lawn. No cover. But at least there were no windows. He came to a thick row of areca palms that formed a barrier along the side of the terrace and pool.

Peering through the fronds, Kozol scouted out the pool. Pamela was there all right. Standing. Wearing a red string bikini.

In one of the loungers nearest the pool, Laura Razner was stretched out topless. Her skin bronze and rich compared to Pamela's own fair skin. Pamela bent over Mrs. Razner and rubbed suntan oil over her supposed rival's stomach and breasts.

Tony was dumbfounded. Could the two of them be lovers?

Pamela leaned over and whispered something in Mrs. Razner's ear.

"No need to lurk in the bushes, Mister Kozol. Come, join us."

Tony pushed his way through the thick palms.

"Hi, baby," said Pamela. "Didn't expect to see you again so soon."

"How did you know I was here?"

Mrs. Razner smiled and tucked a fluffy pink towel up under her armpits. "Amy, that's the guard you so blatantly ignored, she telephoned us as soon as you—broke through," said Mrs. Razner, after a pause. "She was quite insistent about phoning the police."

131

Kozol's neck itched at the thought. Expecting the police was like waiting for the guillotine's blade to fall.

"Don't worry." Laura Razner took a sip of iced tea. "I told her that was not necessary. It isn't, is it, Mister Kozol?"

Pamela walked to the house and Tony heard a car pull away. Pamela returned and took a seat under the covered patio. So someone had left the house but it wasn't her.

"What can I do for you, Tony?"

"I want to know what your husband and my uncle had in common."

Laura Razner laughed. She wordlessly offered Kozol a glass of tea. He declined. "You want to know what my husband and your uncle had in common, Mister Kozol?"

Tony said, "I believe that was the question."

"Money." She dropped the towel as if daring Kozol not to stare at her. Tony wondered if Laura had gone to the same charm school as Pamela. Mrs. Razner draped the towel over the lounger and stretched out on her stomach.

"What does that mean?"

"Oh, let's stop playing games, Tony. Surely you know that your uncle got the money to buy his restaurant from Michael? Michael has been making him pay ever since—"

"That's crazy. Why would Uncle Jonathan borrow money from a guy like Razner?"

"Who knows? Jonathan needed money to start his business. Maybe he couldn't get a bank loan or raise the money through any other more—" Mrs. Razner hesitated, "legitimate means."

"And Razner gave him the money?"

She smiled a wicked, worldly smile. "Gave is hardly

the word I would choose."

"A loan shark?" Kozol asked. Could his God fearing uncle possibly have done such a thing?

"Don't look so surprised, Tony. Plenty of men find themselves in positions quite similar to Jonathan's. Michael simply takes—took—advantage of them."

And maybe Uncle Jonathan got tired of paying and decided that a little revenge was in order before leaving on his cruise. The quicker Kozol found Uncle Jonathan, the better. Not that Tony was going to accept Razner's widow's word for anything but Uncle Jonathan had some explaining to do.

Kozol took a shot. "So when are you moving?"

"Where did you hear that?" Now Laura looked annoyed. She propped herself up on her elbows. Her breasts popped up from their hiding places.

"Word gets around." It was Tony's turn to grin.

"I've gotten sick of living here. Too many memories of my dear husband, as you can imagine. Michael bought us a lovely home over in Jamaica. We never had the chance to share it. Now perhaps there I shall find peace and mend my heart."

So, Mrs. Razner had known all about the Jamaica house. Either that or Pamela had told her about it. Before or after Razner's death? "I'd say you were well on your way," Kozol replied, casting his eye at Pamela.

"Pamela has been a dear," replied Laura, with a grin as enigmatic as the Mona Lisa's.

Tony wondered just how dear. Could there really be a relationship between the two women? Was Laura Razner for all her talk a lesbian or bisexual? Pamela might have had a relationship with each of the Razner's, Michael and Laura. The world was crazier than he thought.

Kozol decided to take another approach. "Don't you think Pamela might have shot your husband?"

"Pamela works in a very public profession. Her whereabouts are well accounted for. I'm afraid you're the only real suspect."

Tony said, "No. I didn't kill anybody. And I can prove it."

"Oh?" said Laura with apparent interest. "How's that?"

"I don't know yet," Kozol confessed. "But I'll let you know."

THIRTEEN

Kozol left Razner's house with more questions than answers. He headed up Lake Drive and drove north. About a mile up the road he noticed the battered red pickup behind him. Riding his tail.

Tony cursed. He hated people who did that. The truck's windshield was filthy, but Kozol could make out somebody in a gray t-shirt and a cowboy hat behind the wheel. There was a lot of oncoming traffic, but in a lull, Tony slowed and motioned for the driver of the pickup to pass him. The driver didn't.

"Idiot," muttered Kozol.

There was another break in the traffic and the pickup pulled up alongside Tony's Saab. The vehicle was an older F-150 with tinted windows. The truck swerved and banged into the Saab.

"Hey!" shouted Kozol, "watch out!" There was no room to maneuver. The pickup blocked him on the left.

To the right there was about a ten foot swale of grass and then a wide drainage canal, one of countless that crisscrossed Florida. The pickup hit him twice in quick succession.

Hard.

Tony was losing control of the Saab. The car spun out sharply to the right and Kozol felt himself traveling upside down. The Saab hit the water as if the surface were made of concrete. It paused there, wheels up and spinning, the stench of burning rubber fouling the air, for several seconds, then quickly began sinking into the murky greenish-brown channel.

Aching and panicky, Tony struggled to release his seat belt and open the door. Even though the car was submerged and the pressure should have equalized, the door wouldn't budge. The pickup had probably damaged it. Kozol scrambled and tried to raise his head. He swallowed water and barely noticed how bad it tasted.

Tony felt the car tilting toward the right and remembered the busted window on that side. He twisted through the opening while the car was still rolling. Another few seconds and his only exit would have been sealed against the muddy bottom.

Kozol's head broke the surface and he scrambled onto the topmost surface of the Saab which was itself a couple of feet below the water line.

"You okay?" cried an elderly gentleman from the bank.

Tony nodded and held on. It was as close to death as he ever wanted to come.

In moments the police had arrived.

"Hold on!" hollered the buzz cut young police officer.

"Fire Rescue is on the way. You hurt? Break anything?"

"Just my baby," groaned Kozol.

"Baby! Jesus, you got a baby in there?"

"No!" Tony hastily explained. "I meant my car."

"Yeah," grinned the officer insensibly. "She's a goner all right."

Fire Rescue arrived and a well rehearsed crew tossed him a line. Moments later, Officer Keyes showed up and took charge over the scene.

"What are you doing here?"

"Got the call on the radio. Anything that concerns you, I get involved."

"Lucky me."

"So," said Officer Keyes, his hands folded stiffly across his broad chest, "having trouble staying on the road?"

Kozol wrapped a thick green towel over his shoulders. One of his rescuers had given it to him to stave off the chills and warned him about the danger of shock setting in.

Tony had shrugged off a trip to the hospital despite the medic's advice. Kozol didn't think there was any real damage to himself, though in spite of the heat he was chilled to the bone.

"Very funny," said Tony. "You taking comic lessons from Frank Fender now?" When Keyes didn't answer Kozol filled the void. "Somebody tried to kill me."

"How's that?" said Officer Keyes, idly scratching his head.

"By running me off the road and into the canal, that's how!"

"You could have lost control of your car. Happens a lot

down here. It's hot. The mind wanders."

"I did not lose control. That is, not until I was bumped. Maybe now you'll take me seriously when I tell you that I didn't kill anybody. Somebody killed Michael Razner and Roamie and now they're out to get me because they figure I'm getting close."

"And are you?" asked Officer Keyes.

"Well, no," admitted Tony. "But I've got a few suspects. Like Pamela Brown or even Laura Razner. I just came from Laura Razner's house, in fact."

"Oh yeah," said Keyes with a thick layer of sarcasm, "those are two mean looking specimens, all right. Together they just might be able to lift a bag of marshmallows. Which one of those bruisers would you say tossed Razner's corpse over her back and stuffed him in the freezer, Kozol?"

"Very funny. Say what you want, but Pamela could have set me up. It wouldn't be the first time."

"Are you saying she did this?"

"No. I guess not. But there was a Cadillac in the garage when I arrived at Razner's house. It was gone when I left."

"Miss Brown drive a Cadillac?"

"No."

"That the alleged vehicle that ran you off the road?"

"Well, no," confessed Kozol, wishing now that he'd never mentioned it. "It was a pickup truck, a big, dirty one."

Officer Keyes left. "Oh yeah. A big, dirty pickup truck. That'd be suspicious all right."

"Surely you saw it?" Tony demanded of the old man who'd first stopped to see if he was all right.

The old fellow leaned against his own vehicle. "No, sorry," said the gentleman. "All I saw was that car of yours flipping over and hitting the water. Figured you were a goner, I did."

Kozol whipped back around to face Officer Keyes squarely. "I'm telling you there was a pickup truck. It was red and there was somebody inside. And he or she was wearing a hat."

Officer Keyes asked, "Did you get a plate number?"

"No, it was an F-150 though."

"Well," conceded Officer Keyes, "I'll arrange for the city to tow out your car. The lab might be able to tell us if you were hit—paint chips and all that. And I'll put out an APB for a red F-150."

"Great."

" Wait'll Detective Fender gets word on this," said the officer, shaking his head from side to side. "He's gonna have a fit. You want a lift?"

"Yeah," said Tony. "You can drop me off at Dairy Delites."

"Sure thing."

Kozol stood shivering while Officer Keyes took the old man's statement and sent him on his way.

"He didn't have much to tell," Officer Keyes said. "He saw the Saab hit the water like he said, and you pop up a minute later. Are you sure you weren't just trying to end it all back there? You know," said Keyes, "the weight of the murders. Maybe it finally got to you. You have a guilty conscience, Kozol?"

"No," Tony answered with annoyance.

Officer Keyes shrugged and handed Kozol a ticket as

they hopped into the cruiser.

"What's this for?" Kozol asked, eyes and mouth wide in astonishment.

"Reckless driving, destruction of public property—" Officer Keyes rattled off matter-of-factly, "and parking in a canal."

"You must be kidding? I was almost killed back there."

"I know," said Officer Keyes. He shifted the car into drive. "But don't worry, I'm not writing you up for that." They slowly merged into traffic, kicking up a trail of gravel that bounced off the underside of the car with an annoying ping.

Tony stared at the small print on the ticket. "What's the destruction of public property citation for?"

"You ran over a speed limit sign back there," Officer Keyes explained. "You know how much those things cost?"

Kozol closed his eyes. He hoped that Uncle Jonathan and Aunt Louise were having the time of their lives on their once-in-a-lifetime vacation. Because as soon as Uncle Jonathan got home, Tony was going to kill him.

FOURTEEN

Business was dead.

Kozol closed the place up at nine o'clock and sent everybody home, figuring he could save a few dollars on the payroll. Nina had barely spoken to him even when he'd told her, and everyone else who would listen, how he'd almost been killed.

Miss Lasher had hardly paid attention at all. Tony got the impression she was mad about something but he couldn't imagine what. After all, he was the one with all the troubles.

He turned off all the lights downstairs, leaving only the outside Dairy Delites neon sign shining out front. Cheap advertising, even if the place was closed for the night.

Kozol went upstairs, determined to put the day behind him. He wanted to get a look at what Nina had been working on. By now, the books and records should have been taking shape. Besides, maybe if he dug around Tony

141

could find something in his uncle's office to tie Jonathan to Razner. What was their connection?

After an hour of futility, pouring over meaningless figures and countless invoices, interspersed with out-of-date supply catalogs which Uncle Jonathan had never gotten around to disposing of, Kozol turned off the desk lamp and collapsed on the sofa. Sleep itself would be an accomplishment at this point.

He set his aim no higher. The sofa was sagging at either end and the lusty scent of Pamela's perfume still pervaded the cushions. Tony closed his eyes and thought of those lips.

Kozol woke in a sweat and sat up quickly. The strangeness of his surroundings frightened him until he remembered he was still in the upstairs office. Tony heard a muffled noise downstairs. So that was what woke him.

He rose slowly. The tiny clock on the desk was lighted. It read twelve-thirteen. Tony wondered who the hell could be downstairs at that time of night. He heard the sound again. It sounded like footsteps, and metal on metal.

Kozol cautiously turned the door knob and pulled open the door ever so slightly. Ever so slowly. It creaked anyway. The sounds stopped.

"Hey! Who's down there?" Tony called out, summoning all his courage for one big challenge.

The sound of something falling and then quick foot steps receding.

He gripped the door and shouted shakily, "What do you think you're doing down there? What do you want?" There was no reply. Tony hadn't expected one.

STIFF IN THE FREEZER

Kozol tumbled down the stairs in the darkness. He bumped into something, then discovered it was a someone when whoever it was grunted. In frightened surprise, he cried out, "Hey!"

Tony grabbed what felt like a coat. He pulled! The invisible stranger pushed Kozol away with a sharp thrust to the ribs and broke free!

The back door shot open and the dark figure ran past him, puffing. Tony hesitated, then gave chase but the mysterious figure had disappeared into the shadows.

Kozol made his way cautiously back inside, fearful there might be a cohort of the escaped burglar lurking inside, perhaps waiting to pounce from behind the door.

Tony turned on the back lights with a shaky hand. The floor safe was untouched. He inspected the back door. The lock wasn't broken. Whoever had gotten in was either an expert locksmith or had the key.

Either way, Kozol was going to get the locks changed. The last thing he needed was a break-in. He wasn't even certain if the equipment was insured against loss.

He checked the locks on all the doors and left all the lights on as he went. Tony didn't think whoever broke in would try again that night, but he wasn't taking any chances. He propped a stool up against the back door and set a metal mixing bowl on top the stool. It wouldn't keep anybody out but it would make some noise if anybody tried to get in through the back again.

Kozol slipped in a puddle of grease as he headed back to the stairs and decided he'd cuss Joe out in the morning for not mopping up properly.

¤

The pounding slowly filtered up from below. Tony dreamt of police banging down his door and hauling him off to jail.

The pounding grew louder and Kozol woke.

It was morning. He was stiff and, instead of standing straight up, clumsily rolled off the couch and hit the floor. "Ooof!" he groaned. "All right, all right!" he shouted out. "I'm coming."

Tony rose and oriented himself. Somebody was at the back door.

Kozol pushed aside the stool and opened the door.

Joe burst in. "It's about time. I've been knocking for ten minutes. Man," said Joe, "what happened to you?"

Tony looked down at his rumpled clothes and rubbed his unshaven jaw. "I fell asleep upstairs. I was—"

Nina came in through the open door and passed between Tony and Joe without making the least bit of eye contact. "Morning," she said frostily.

"Hey," said Joe.

Kozol reached out his hand and stopped her. "Is everything all right?"

"Yes, fine," she said, tossing off Tony's hand.

"Are you sure?" Kozol pressed. "You seem upset about something."

"Uh-oh," Joe said.

Tony said, "Don't you have some work to do? Like mopping the floor?"

Joe looked aggrieved. "I mopped up last night, front to back. Ask anybody."

"Well, I almost broke my neck stepping in that grease behind you. You probably spilled it carrying the grease filters."

"Hey, I put those filters in the can before I mopped."

The can was a fifty-five gallon drum which the grease filters soaked in overnight. They had two sets of filters. While one was in place over the grill, the other was soaking.

Joe started fishing the filters out of the greasy, brown sludge with a pair of pliers they kept for that purpose.

"Can I go now?" Nina asked.

"Wait. Tell me what's wrong first," Kozol insisted.

"I told you, nothing is wrong Mister Kozol," she said with particular emphasis. "I have work to do. That's what you pay me for. If you want to have a conversation why don't you call Miss-I'm-So-Gorgeous the stripper!"

Tony said, "What are you talking about? You mean Pamela?"

"Yes, Pamela. You know, the girl who helped get you disbarred and you still can't keep your hands off—"

"Pamela doesn't mean anything to me," Kozol tried to explain.

"Oh, I see," Nina said. "So the two of you were screwing on the upstairs sofa just for the hell of it!"

"Joe!" Tony growled, angrily turning on the young man.

"I didn't know it was some kind of a secret, boss," Joe replied defensively.

"So you decided to tell the world?"

Joe said nothing, having apparently decided it was finally time to shut up.

Nina turned and started to leave.

Once again Kozol reached out to stop her. Nina turned and raised her arms. "Don't touch me!" she said with mounting indignation.

She pushed.

Tony fell into Joe's back. Joe slipped in the puddle of grease still on the floor and he dropped the pliers. They sunk slowly to the bottom of the vat. "Now look what you made me do!" Joe said.

"What?" said Kozol, still in shock from Nina's rage. Was this really about Pamela?

"I dropped the pliers," Joe said.

"So reach in and get them."

"I'm not sticking my hand into that thing!" Joe said. "You know how much gunk is down there?"

"Oh, please," Tony said, clearly annoyed. "Get something long, maybe a spatula and see if you can scoop them up then."

"Let's buy some new pliers, boss."

"Forget it. I can't afford to spend any more money than I have to. In fact, if you're lucky, maybe you'll find some loose change rattling around in there under all that gook. I'll split it with you, fifty-fifty. Who knows? Maybe you'll even find the murder weapon. Then you'd really be doing me a favor—"

"Oh, all right," grumbled Joe, his fingers hovering undecidedly over the greasy water.

"Wait!" shouted Nina.

"What?" Kozol looked at Nina. "What's wrong?"

"What you just said."

"What did I just say?"

"Never mind," said Nina. "Tell Joe to forget about the pliers. We'll get them later."

"Why?"

Nina kissed Tony on the mouth. "Because I think you're brilliant," she said. "Come on."

When Kozol didn't move, Nina pushed his thunder-struck body up the stairs. She closed the door behind them. "I have an idea," she said.

Tony listened.

FIFTEEN

"**O**uch!"

"Huh? What's wrong?"

"You hit me in the head with your elbow," Nina whispered crossly.

"Sorry, I must have dozed off." Kozol was feeling tired and miserable. He and Nina were lying perched upon the top of the walk-in refrigerator wherein they stored the fresh produce and dairy products.

There was a space a couple of feet high at best between the top of the refrigerator and the ceiling. Big enough for them to stretch out on, but uncomfortably hard and hot. And covered with dust and twenty year old cobwebs.

Tony groaned. "We should have brought sleeping bags."

"What, and nice comfy pillows?"

"Very funny," whispered Kozol. "I don't think this idea of yours is going to work anyway." He looked at his watch. "It's nearly two a.m. And I'm hungry."

Nina propped herself up on her elbows. "I don't understand. I can't be wrong." She glared at Tony through the dim ambient light. "Are you certain you gave Miss Brown the message like I told you to?"

Kozol huffed. "Of course I'm sure. I telephoned Pamela from my apartment. I told her I had figured out where the gun was that killed Razner and that I was going to get it tomorrow, then turn it over to the police."

Nina nodded.

"You still think she's going to show up here tonight and try to get the gun?"

"Yes. It's human nature. After all, Pamela doesn't know if you're on to her or not. But if Miss Brown dropped the gun in the grease drum, she's going to figure this might be her last chance to get it back."

"Why on earth would she put it there in the first place?"

"Who knows?" Nina sounded annoyed. "Maybe she got scared or maybe she figured it was as good a place as any to hide a gun until she could dispose of it for good."

"Face it," said Tony, "you could be wrong about her."

"Men," said Nina in disgust. "You should try thinking with your head instead of your—thing."

"What's that supposed to mean?"

"It means I'm trying to keep you from going to jail, you idiot! And you've got the hots for our best suspect. Pamela was having an affair with Razner. He probably threatened to break it off with her. I think he wanted to go to Jamaica for good. Miss Brown couldn't stand giving up that easy money. She either followed him here or came with him, saw her opportunity and took it."

"I'm still not so sure—"

"Look how she's fawning all over Laura Razner now. Pamela even told Mrs. Razner about the Jamaica house. She's a hussy. A hussy and a gold digger," pronounced Nina, firmly.

"I resent that idiot remark."

"Sorry," Nina said, though she hadn't sounded like she meant it.

"And I don't have the hots for Pamela." Kozol knew this wasn't exactly true but Nina was getting on his nerves. "She came on to me."

"Oh, you poor baby."

Tony scowled. "I don't know why I even talk to you. Every time I—"

"Shhh—" Miss Lasher put her hand on Kozol's shoulder. "Did you hear that?"

"I didn't hear anything," Tony answered sourly.

"Shush. Not so loud," admonished Nina.

Kozol peered into the gloom. Though he had to credit Miss Lasher with deciding to stake out the restaurant from the vantage point of the walk-in, her plan had so far been a disaster.

Tony could barely make out the walls and counters. Shadows merged with darkness. There was nothing to see.

And suddenly the back door was open.

Kozol froze. He felt Nina's nails digging into his shoulder and suppressed his need to yelp. She pushed his head down.

The dark figure closed the door silently and paused for only a moment before heading for the big grease drum in the corner. It was still too dark to see. The figure could have been a woman but there was no way to tell for sure.

Another flaw in their plan. He should have picked up some night vision binoculars and a flashlight.

Tony heard faint clacking and sloshing sounds. If Nina was right, whoever had killed Michael Razner had hidden the weapon in the grease barrel. If so, Pamela was trying to retrieve the gun now.

Kozol put his mouth to Nina's ear. "Now what?"

Miss Lasher shrugged. "Call the police?"

"Gee, excuse me while I look for a phone booth." He gave Miss Lasher's ear a playful lick knowing full well she dare not expose them. "Any other ideas?"

She pulled him by the nose with a vise-like grip. His eyes watered up. "I guess you'll just have to go down there and apprehend Miss Brown."

"Me. By the time I—"

Nina clamped her hand over Tony's mouth and pointed.

The door was opening again.

The figure near the drum froze.

The lights came on.

Kozol couldn't help shouting, "Uncle Jonathan!"

SIXTEEN

And Laura Razner. Holding a dripping gun. She aimed first at Jonathan Kozol and pulled the trigger but the gun, soaking wet and coated with congealed fat, refused to fire. She threw it and ran.

In the meantime, Nina had pushed Tony into action. Literally. She gave him a shove that sent him over the top of the walk-in. Kozol hit the big ice machine below and bounced heavily to the floor.

"Grab her!" shouted Nina. "Don't let her get away!"

Tony glanced up. Between the spinning room and the dancing stars he saw Mrs. Razner running into the dining room. Uncle Jonathan was quickly making for the back door. "Uncle Jonathan! Stop! Wait!"

Kozol scrambled to his feet. He ran clumsily after his uncle who had already made the door.

Tony ran madly past the counter and might have caught up with his uncle but for one thing—Razner's widow hadn't been too careful in her search. Kozol slipped in a puddle of greasy water and bounced hip first off the door. He cried out in pain.

"Get up! Everybody's getting away!" scolded Miss Lasher.

"I'm trying," whined Tony. He rubbed his hip. "I think I might have broken something."

"Oh, please. Do I have to come down there and do everything?"

"That would be nice." Kozol rolled onto his knees.

Detective Fender kicked open the door and came in. He had his hand around Uncle Jonathan's neck.

"Uncle Jonathan!"

"Hey, kiddo."

"You've got to get Mrs. Razner," Nina said. "She ran out that way!"

"Don't worry, lady."

Laura Razner soon came through the door escorted by Officer Keyes and two other officers whom Tony didn't recognize. "This is absurd," said Mrs. Razner, struggling to loosen the officer's grip.

"I agree," said Fender. "I hate being up at two in the morning." He looked to Miss Lasher. "You need any help getting down from there?"

"No, we've put a ladder on the other side."

Kozol approached his uncle. "Uncle Jonathan, what's going on? You're supposed to be on a cruise. You don't know what kind of trouble I've been in."

"I'm sorry, Tony. I didn't mean to involve you. It's all her fault," he said, casting an accusing eye toward Laura Razner.

"What do you mean?"

"She killed her husband. Right here," Uncle Jonathan explained. "I saw her do it. She didn't know it was me, though. You see, Razner was meeting me here that night. He wanted money—cash. Said he was going to get away for good. Said it would be the last time. The bastard had been bleeding me dry for years."

"So that's why he came here?"

"Yeah," said Uncle Jonathan. "Making me pay through the teeth for the money I'd borrowed from him to start this place. Anyway, he had a briefcase full of money. I took it."

"You mean there was no inheritance?" asked Nina.

"That's right. You see, I paid him off like he wanted. Then Razner said he wanted to make some calls. Probably to the rest of the suckers he was going to collect from. I told him to lock up when he was finished and I left."

"I have to warn you that anything you say—" Detective Fender began.

"I know, I know." Uncle Jonathan paused while Officer Keyes read off his rights. "You finished?"

Keyes nodded.

"Anyway, I was just pulling out of the lot when I saw Razner's wife lurking about. That made me curious. I mean, he never brings her with him. Sometimes a girlfriend, but never his wife. So I left my car up the road and came back. When I got here I heard Razner and his wife arguing."

"Oh, do shut up!" pleaded Laura.

Uncle Jonathan ignored her. "She was mad as hell. He tried to reason with her. I got a kick out of that. The next thing I know, Razner turns around, picks up the briefcase and makes to leave. Cool as anything, Laura pulls out a gun and shoots the bastard."

Uncle Jonathan wavered. "That scared me, I don't mind telling you. That scared me bad. I must have gasped or something because she heard the sound. I saw Laura toss the gun in the drum and run out."

"He's making this all up!" exclaimed Mrs. Razner. "I loved my husband."

"Maybe that's it. You loved him too much. You were afraid of losing him," Nina said.

Laura gave her no answer.

Uncle Jonathan said, "When I was sure Laura was gone I picked up the briefcase. I stuffed Razner's body in a box and thought I'd buried him safely in the back of the freezer. Hell, there's boxes that have been untouched for years back there. I didn't think he'd be found for a long time to come. And maybe I could dispose of him before that ever happened at all. Same with the gun."

"Jesus," said Kozol. "Why didn't you call the police?"

Uncle Jonathan looked at his feet. "All that money," he confessed. "Over a million bucks in cash inside that briefcase. It was too much for me to resist. You do understand, don't you, Tony? I never meant for any of it to come back on you."

"Tony was arrested for murder," said Nina. "How could you do that to him?"

"I know, I know." Uncle Jonathan pulled himself free from Detective Fender's grasp. "That's why I tried to make it right. I stuck around and sent your aunt off on the cruise. I told her I'd catch up to her as quick as I could after helping you get started here at the restaurant."

Uncle Jonathan covered his face with his hands and cried. "God, I screwed up."

"So," said Nina, "that's what your wife's postcard meant about the two of you getting along. She thought you were here helping Tony."

Uncle Jonathan nodded.

"What about Roamie?" demanded Fender.

"Yes," said Laura, breaking her icy silence, "you like to talk so much, Jonathan, do please tell us about Roamie." She gave Jonathan a look a black widow spider would have admired.

Uncle Jonathan whispered, "I had to kill him."

"No," said Kozol, taking a step back. First stolen money and now murder. Surely his uncle had gone mad.

"I had to," said Uncle Jonathan, wringing his hands. "He saw me. You see, I came back one night after Razner's murder. I wanted to get the gun and throw it in the ocean. Roamie saw me.

At first I thought he was only scrounging around for some food. But then he told me that he had seen me the night Razner was killed—the nosey fool. If only he'd minded his own business, Roamie would still be alive.

He tried to blackmail me and said he would tell the police what he saw if I didn't give him money. I pretended to go along and then—"

"You cut his throat," Nina said, dispassionately.

Kozol's own throat was constricted and he could barely speak. "No, Uncle Jonathan, tell me you didn't."

"He did," said Laura, with apparent glee. "And I was watching. I suspected it was Jonathan who had witnessed

Michael's death and kept an eye on him."

"So you planted the knife in Tony's apartment?" Nina asked.

Laura nodded.

"When I read in the newspaper about the knife being found in your apartment, I knew we were both in trouble, Tony," said Uncle Jonathan. "And Laura and I have been playing cat and mouse ever since. That's how I happened to follow her here tonight."

Uncle Jonathan looked at his nephew as if asking for mercy. "I was still trying to make everything right."

Kozol didn't know how to respond. "That was you I caught in here the other night?"

"Yes."

"And did you try to run Tony off the road, too?" demanded Nina.

"Of course not."

"Then it had to be Mrs. Razner or one of her cohorts," Nina spoke. "She probably planted the fifty thousand dollars in your account as well, Tony."

Officer Keyes nodded. "We traced that pickup. It belonged to one of Razner's bouncers. He'll talk soon enough."

Laura Razner stood silently, as if struggling to maintain her dignity.

"We've had a tail on her ever since."

"So that's what you're doing here." Tony looked at his poor uncle. Things were falling into place and it wasn't pretty.

"I don't think you'll get much out of her," opined Detective Fender. "Mrs. Razner doesn't look like the confession type."

"With Michael gone, I don't care what happens to me, anymore," said Laura, stoically.

Officer Keyes placed Mrs. Razner in cuffs and led her away.

"I can't believe it," said Kozol, shaking his head. "What happens now?"

"I'd say your uncle here was going to need a good lawyer," said Fender.

"Very funny," said Tony.

"Oh, not so funny. In light of everything that's happened—and I'm no lawyer or judge, mind you—but I'd say you stand a decent chance of being reinstated to the Bar."

"Hey, maybe he's right," Nina said. She gave Kozol a hug.

"Maybe," agreed Tony. He watched as the detective turned his uncle over to the two uniformed officers. "But Joe said I was just getting the hang of flipping a burger."

"It's up to you," said Nina.

More officers arrived to secure the scene. Squad cars with painfully bright red and blue flashers circled the Dairy Delites like land sharks approaching a fresh kill.

A wave of relief washed over Kozol. "Well, that's it. I guess this let's me off the hook. And Pamela. I told you, Nina, that you were wrong about her."

Detective Fender looked from his ex-prime suspect to Miss Lasher. "If you would like to punch this idiot in the nose, I'd be happy to look the other way."

Tony hastily assessed the look in Miss Lasher's eye, the angle of moment, the force of Coulomb's law as it might apply to the electricity between their two bodies, the entire energy-mass relationship which constrains the cosmos, the kinetic energy massed in her mean looking knuckles and the tonal qualities of bone striking cartilage.

Kozol did the addition. One plus one did indeed equal two. Quickly he kissed her. A tactical, preemptive first strike.

Nina drew back, smiled, her right hand poised in the shape of a fist, and declared, "I'll take a rain check."